Fantastic Four®

MARVEL COMICS

Fantastic Four®

TO FREE Atlantis

Nancy A. Collins

Illustrations by Paul Ryan

MARVEL COMICS

BYRON PREISS MULTIMEDIA COMPANY, INC.
New York

BOULEVARD BOOKS
New York

Special thanks to Lou Aronica, Ginjer Buchanan, Ken Grobe, Julia Molino, Stacy Gittelman, and the gang at Marvel Creative Services.

FANTASTIC FOUR: TO FREE ATLANTIS

A Boulevard Book
A Byron Preiss Multimedia Company, Inc. Book

PRINTING HISTORY
Boulevard edition / December 1995

ISBN: 1-57297-054-5

BOULEVARD
Boulevard Books are published by The Berkley Publishing Group,
200 Madison Avenue, New York, New York 10016.
BOULEVARD and its logo
are trademarks belonging to Berkley Publishing Corporation.

PRINTED IN THE UNITED STATES OF AMERICA

10   9   8   7   6   5   4   3   2   1

This book is written in the spirit of the Fantastic Four's fifth teammate, Jack "King" Kirby, and the true Lord of Atlantis, Bill Everett. Thanks for the rainy day fun, guys.

The author would like to acknowledge the following source material concerning the lifestyles of emperors and the origins of Atlantis: *Claudius the God* by Robert Graves, *The Who's Who of Ancient Greek and Roman Mythology*, and *The Twelve Caesars* by Suetonius.

Listen and appear to us
In name of great Oceanus,
By the earth-shaking Neptune's mace,
And Tethys' grave majestic pace,
By hoary Nereus' wrinkled look,
And the Carpathian wizard's hook,
By scaly Triton's winding shell,
And old sooth-saying Glaucus' spell,
By Leucothea's lovely hands,
And her son that rules the strands,
By Thetis' tinsel-slippered feet,
And the songs of sirens sweet,
By dead Parthenope's dear tomb,
And fair Ligea's golden comb,
Wherewith she sits on diamond rocks
Sleeking her soft alluring locks . . .

—John Milton, from "A Mask
Presented at Ludlow Castle [Comus]"

CHAPTER 1

A DAY IN THE LIFE OF THE SUB-MARINER

Seen from the far reaches of space, the planet called Earth seems to be a world made of water. On closer inspection, although continents can be discerned, the oceans that blanket the globe are indeed vast, covering 140 million square miles—nearly seventy-one percent of the surface.

Beneath the water's restless waves is a universe glimpsed rarely by those who dwell on land. At first it seems horribly alien to human eyes. There is no day or night, nor even any seasons, as we have come to understand them. Compared to the verdant fields and forest glens of the surface world, the sea mounts and steep hills that cover most of the ocean floor seem sterile and foreboding. But once the initial shock of the new wears off, visitors become aware of the marvels that surround them.

There are fish of every possible shape and color, flashing and glittering like jewels tossed into the surf; an infinite variety of jellyfish, as beautiful as they are deadly, placidly riding the currents like discarded balloons; schools of sea mammals as diverse as the fun-loving sea otters and the lordly blue whales. And there are fearsome things lurking in the ocean's depths as well—things that are all teeth and appetite, whose basic predatory design has remained unchanged for millions of years.

But not all things found in the oceans are of Nature's design. Scattered along the floor of the various seas and gulfs that comprise the bodies of water that wrap the planet like a mother's arms can be found the handiwork of human beings. Indeed, the history of humanity can be traced by its traditional shipping lanes: the wreck of a Spanish galleon lies beside the barnacle-encrusted ruin of a Viking reaver, which rests scant yards from a torpedoed British freighter, which all but obscures the remains of a downed American bomber.

Oh, yes—and there are cities below the sea.

These underwater cities lay miles below the surface, far from prying eyes, where the pressure is so great it can crush a person's insides. But while they are, in their way, secret communities, they are far from unknown. Indeed, the name of the greatest of these drowned metropolises is familiar even to landlocked humans who have lived and died without once setting eyes on the great water from whence their kind first emerged, countless aeons past.

This city was once the gleaming jewel of the Ancient World, a land of powerful magic and technological marvels, the capital of a legendary island kingdom where sorcery and technology grew side-by-side, until one was indistinguishable from the other. It was the birthplace of heroes and princes said to be descended from the ten sons sired by Poseidon on a mortal woman—

—and was obliterated from the face of the Earth over ten thousand years ago by a catastrophe unparalleled in history.

Atlantis.

Many call it a myth. Others have called it an allegory—a cautionary fable used to instruct against the folly of pride and impiety.

But a select few call it "home."

* * *

The denizens of lost Atlantis were once, long centuries ago, creatures of the light and air. And some habits are very hard to break. So there is the Royal Timekeeper, whose job it is to monitor the pale and distant sun, and sound the trumpet from the battlements to mark its rising and its setting.

And with the morning call, so another day comes to Atlantis, and to its sovereign: Namor I, known to the people of the surface world as the Sub-Mariner.

"Good morning, my liege," said Vashti, the Chief Court Chamberlain, as he drew apart the heavy sealskin draperies of the royal bed fashioned from a clamshell large enough to swallow a grown man whole.

"Good morning, old friend," yawned Namor as he sat up and stretched, casually displaying a physique that made classical statues seem puny. At six feet three inches and over seventy years of age—not even middle-aged, by Atlantean standards—Namor was as strong as a hundred of his most vigorous subjects. And, since even the most ordinary of Atlantean citizens was as strong as an elephant, it was easy to see how Namor came to be regarded as one of the planet's mightiest mortals.

But it was not merely in matters of physical prowess that Namor differed from his subjects. Although the blood in his veins was indeed royal—his family claimed direct descent from the god Poseidon himself—Namor was unlike any other Atlantean born. While most merhumans had blue skin, Namor's was pink. And although he shared their pointed ears, upswept eyebrows, and longevity, he also possessed winged ankles—like those once said to have belonged to the gods of old—that allowed him to fly through both air and sea, and, unlike any of his kinsmen, he was capable of breathing air as easily as he could water. The reason for these differences had to do with his parentage. For while his mother was Atlantean, his father had been human.

As a youth, Namor had been teased by his playmates and called, amongst many things, a "hybrid," "throwback," and "mutant"—all true, to some degree or other. But that was before he became ruler. And if any of his subjects still thought him a freak, they wisely kept it to themselves.

Vashti clapped his hands and motioned for the Grand Master of the Wardrobe to bring him the prince's dressing gown. "Would you have me recite the day's schedule, Your Highness?" he asked as he helped Namor into the robe.

"Do I have a choice, Vashti?" Namor chuckled. The Chief Court Chamberlain was an elderly Atlantean of noble lineage, his long beard and tangled mane gone gray in service of the royal family. He had served Namor's mother, Queen Fen, and her father before her, King Nereus XXIII. Indeed, there was no time in Namor's memory when Vashti had not been on hand. The old man was the closest thing he'd had to a father growing up. And although the Chamberlain was easily older than a century or more, his mind was as sharp as a shark's tooth, his wisdom unparalleled.

Vashti produced a small scroll from a voluminous sleeve. "Today you are to attend a pantomime performed by the Ithkar IX Memorial Nursery Pod, hear appeals to the Royal Court, and induct Hiordis as a Lord of the Realm." Finished, he returned the scroll to its hiding place and motioned once again to the Master of the Wardrobe, who scuttled forward, a bottle of cologne held on a golden serving platter for the Chamberlain's inspection. Satisfied that the proffered scent was indeed of the finest grade, Vashti placed a few well-placed drops on Namor's hands and hair.

"Really, Vashti," Namor sighed. "Must we go through this rigamarole every morning? I could dress and groom myself much faster . . ."

"I know you have no patience for the rituals of station, my prince. I blame that on your exposure to the surface world. You've spent far too much time with air-breathers. Especially the ones called 'Americans.' They have proven a bad influence on you, if you would allow me such familiarity, Your Highness."

"My father was an American sailor, Vashti—"

"And your mother was an Atlantean princess! You have obligations to the throne and the crown, Namor. I have made allowances for your nature, such as your insistence on abandoning the use of the royal 'we' in your speech. Why, your grandfather had sixty-seven Royal Supervisors, forty-two Lord Stewards, thirty-one Royal Comptrollers, seventeen Court Chamberlains, and two Lord Chamberlains in his service. But certain rituals *must* be observed if you are to rule! Your subjects expect it. And should your hold on the crown falter for even an instant, there is one who would waste no time in placing it on his brow.''

"You mean Byrrah.''

"I would not presume to speak thus of a prince of the blood.''

It was impossible for Namor not to laugh. "Come now, Vashti! You and I both know you can't stand my cousin!''

The Chamberlain was highly embarrassed, but dared not contradict the prince. Vashti's loyalty to the royal family was indeed sincere, and it extended even to those members he personally disliked. Upon seeing his discomfort, Namor immediately regretted the burst of humor at his friend's expense. He smiled kindly and gently clapped the old retainer on his shoulder.

"Forgive me, Vashti. I didn't mean to insult the blood oath you swore upon coming into the service of my grandfather. Come, let us go break my fast! I'll need a fortifying meal of salmon roe and fresh octopus if I am to serve as the Royal Magistrate today!''

"Indeed, Your Highness. Indeed.''

* * *

Namor stepped out onto the balcony that overlooked the Grand Plaza outside the royal palace and was greeted by the fanfare of conches and the cheer of the crowd. Vashti was already awaiting him, his appointment scroll clutched in one hand.

"I trust I am not late," he whispered to the older man as he waved and smiled at the throng below.

"How can you be late? You are the prince. Nothing begins until you have arrived," Vashti remarked curtly.

"That's not what you used to say when I was your student, old friend. Now, refresh my memory—which citizens' group is here to do me honors?"

"The Ithkar IX Memorial Nursery Pod."

"Ah, yes."

A dozen or more young children, dressed in special costumes, were assembled below the balcony. Over the years, the tale of how the Avenging Son returned from his amnesiac exile had become a popular topic for children's pantomime. Namor smiled as a small boy, smeared in special body paint to mimic his own pale flesh color and wearing a beard of seaweed, was accosted by a child dressed all in red, who was supposed to be Johnny Storm. Standing in the wings, awaiting their cues, were two nursery-pod children—a boy and a girl—dressed in blue, in the company of a slightly larger child outfitted in homemade armor cobbled from the carapaces of horseshoe crabs. No doubt they were playing the parts of Storm's teammates: Reed Richards, Susan Storm Richards, and Ben Grimm.

It felt odd to see these scenes from his own life performed before him by children a tenth his age. And as the young performers went through their ritual gestures, Namor found his thoughts drifting back to the events they were re-creating.

It had happened years ago, back when he had wandered amongst his father's people, his memory erased by some trauma he still was unable to recollect. Severed from his past, he degenerated into a pathetic shadow of a man, his hair grown long, his face obscured by a filthy beard. Although he had forgotten his life beneath the waves, some dim spark of awareness kept him close to his native element, even if it was the polluted waters of the Hudson River. He dwelt amongst similar skid-row derelicts—but for how long not even he could say.

It was in a nameless mission located in the Bowery that the youth named Johnny Storm first found him and, miracle of miracles, somehow recognized in the grizzled derelict's features the legendary Sub-Mariner, who had disappeared some time after the Second World War. Then again, perhaps it was not so strange that the boy had discovered him. After all, fire calls to water, sky to earth. And was not Johnny Storm better known as the Human Torch?

It was Johnny's idea to jar Namor's memory by dropping him into the cold, dark waters of New York's Hudson River. In many ways, Johnny Storm reminded Namor of himself in younger days: brash, callow, quick to anger, even quicker to fight. It had never occurred to the boy that the Sub-Mariner's reawakening might be far more traumatic than simply rousing him from a long nap.

As he plummeted to the bottom of the river, the amnesiac Namor began to panic. He was going to drown! Then, to his amazement, he discovered he could breathe underwater. His memory suddenly came rushing back. However, it returned in somewhat imperfect condition, and when he saw the Human Torch, it was not Johnny Storm he saw.

Many years ago, before Namor lost his memory, there had been another, different, Human Torch—one who blazed through the skies like a comet. One who had used his pyrokinetic powers to fight for justice. During the Sub-Mariner's own rash, headstrong youth, when he was determined to avenge the wrongs done to Atlantis by the surface-dwellers, Namor had battled that other Human Torch on more than one occasion. Their confrontations were epic in scope and devastation, as befits the elements.

In time, he and the Torch turned their animosity away from each other and focused it on the armies of the Axis, even going so far as to band together with other super-powered heroes, such as Captain America, to battle as a team.

But when his memories came back to him piecemeal years later, it was as if the Second World War had never happened and he was once again Prince Namor, Avenging Son of Atlantis. And so the first thing Namor thought, when he saw the boy made of fire hovering in the sky over the river, was that his old foe, the Human Torch, had attacked him once again. Enraged, he launched himself into a battle against what he imagined to be his enemy, which began a history of misunderstandings with the group of super heroes who called themselves the Fantastic Four.

Like the World War II–era Human Torch, the foursome had started off as enemies, but eventually became allies. Although he had been raised to see all air-breathers as evil, Namor had also been taught to respect and value bravery, heroism, and valor, characteristics the Fantastic Four certainly had in abundance. And, in the case of Susan Storm Richards—known to the world as the Invisible Woman—Namor's respect was tempered with a far more tender emotion.

Namor had loved the fair-haired beauty since the moment he first laid eyes on her, and knew, in his heart of hearts, that he would continue loving her until the day his bones became coral. However, Namor's passion was an unrequited one—for her heart would always belong to her husband.

Yet, this knowledge did not lessen how he felt. Over the years his love for Susan had remained, even after her marriage to Reed Richards and the birth of their child, Franklin. Even his own two brief, tragic marriages did little to dampen his passion. No doubt his cousin, Byrrah, would dismiss him as fool for being so enamored of a human female. After all, he was Namor, Prince of Atlantis, Prince of the Seven Seas! He could take as his wife any woman under the waves. Instead he chose to moon over an air-breather.

Namor's reverie was interrupted by the blast of trumpets. The children froze in their reenactment, their eyes suddenly huge as they searched the shadowy depths for signs of danger. The warning trumpets sounded only when the walls of the city were breached by hostile forces. Was it another attack by Attuma's barbarian hordes? Or was it the Lemurians this time? Perhaps the attacker was a kraken?

Namor got his answer as he glimpsed the monstrous shadow cutting through the water with the speed of a torpedo, attracted by the children's colorful costumes and the sounds of their laughter.

"*Shark!*"

And a big one, too—at least twenty feet long. The Great White cut through the water like a knife, the snapped haft of a harpoon trailing behind it. The creature had somehow managed to breach the gill nets and elude the harpoon-masters that defended the city from such deep-sea predators.

Namor launched himself at the beast as the children screamed and swam for cover. He caught the shark square in the belly, using his fists like a battering ram. He narrowly avoided the double row of serrated teeth that filled its gaping mouth.

Momentarily dazed, the shark's flat shoe-button eyes showed only mindless fury. The Great White was as fast as a speedboat, but the Sub-Mariner was far more agile. He dodged its strike, digging his powerful fingers into the beast's gill slits as it zipped by. The shark's massive jaws opened even wider as Namor straddled its back, pulling with his bare hands. It thrashed its tail violently back and forth, but there was no way it could unseat its tormentor.

There was no question as to the outcome of the battle, but Namor did not want it to drag on, for fear of harming any of the onlookers. He could not simply snap the shark's back and get it over with, since the creature had no bones to break, and drowning the monster could prove time-consuming, not to mention potentially hazardous to bystanders. Which meant he had only one other recourse.

Namor flexed his legs and with one solid kick was speeding toward the distant surface like a missile, dragging the five-ton shark in his wake as if it weighed no more than a minnow. The shark thrashed as it underwent abrupt, violent decompression, but the Sub-Mariner did not loosen his grip. Suddenly the darkness of the ocean's floor was replaced by the glare and brilliance of the sun, and the Sub-Mariner burst from the blue waters that birthed him, rising from the waterspout like an ancient sea god.

The wings on his heels beating like a hummingbird's, the mighty Sub-Mariner rose high into the cobalt blue sky. The same, however, could not be said of the shark, which twitched and shuddered in his grasp as it began to suffocate. Namor opened his arms and let go of the Great White, which plummeted thirty feet through the air before striking the water, where it sank without a trace.

* * *

Long before the gleaming spires of Atlantis disappeared beneath the waves, it had been the duty of its princes to serve as magistrates once every sixty days, hearing the cases of those citizens who, having exhausted the lesser courts, wished to appeal to the wisdom and judiciousness of their ruler. Except for the odd charge of treason or murder, the docket usually consisted of such mundane matters as disputes over property claims, the division of inheritances, and simple tax evasion.

While Namor was often bored while listening to these petty squabbles, he realized it was a duty he dared not shirk. Atlanteans might be loyal to the crown, but not blindly so. A just ruler who understood and fulfilled his duties to his people would fare better than one who was indolent or cruel. Still, this understanding of what was required did not make the time pass any faster, and Namor found himself longing for another shark to burst through the gill nets to break the monotony.

He had already heard ten appeals when the Royal Bailiff called the eleventh and final case. Namor did his best to stifle a groan when he saw the law-speaker who accompanied the plaintiff. It was Geryon, one of the city-state's most notorious pedants. The case in question had something to do with property boundaries, but the law-speaker's rhetoric was so dense, Namor was lost within seconds of Geryon opening his mouth.

Geryon had several scrolls with him, supposedly relating to the case at hand. Gesturing grandly with one of these, he smiled at Namor and said, "Surely, Your Highness, you are aware of the twenty-sixth subsection of the ninth article of Pontus VI's Law, published in the Year of the Seahorse . . ."

Namor's voice—deep and resonant, used to speaking and being heard—cut the law-speaker short. "You are mistaken, Citizen Geryon. I am quite unaware of my nine-times great grandsire's lawmaking. Unlike yourself, I cannot supply precise legal opinions on any judicial matter under the waves. I am merely the High Judge of Atlantis. But before you go any further, my good law-speaker, allow me to remind you: I detest oratory. I also have no fondness for pointless chatter concerning a plaintiff's ancestral nobility, the number of needy family members dependent on him, and the fickleness of fortune. Nor do I respond favorably to appeals for clemency or flattery concerning my wisdom and merciful nature. If you cannot state your client's case briefly and lucidly, with the necessary witnesses, then I shall levy the stiffest penalty against him, as is permitted in the law, for his dishonesty and your waste of public time. Is *that* understood, Citizen Geryon?"

The law-speaker swallowed and his face went pale. "Y-yes, sir."

Needless to say, Geryon's client lost.

* * *

Though the Congress of Lords was originally founded two hundred centuries ago, it was all but destroyed during the Great Cataclysm that pulled the island kingdom below the waves. When the merhumans set about reconstructing the glory that was Atlantis, the Congress, along with the royal palace and the Temple of Poseidon, was one of the first structures they turned their hands to rebuilding, reconstructing the vast rotunda out of the finest coral available. It was there that the noble lords proposed and argued for and against civil laws and other such public matters.

Only the nobility were allowed to vote, but the common citizenry was permitted to observe from the galleries that lined the walls. The floor of the Congress was dominated by a huge throne—permanently reserved for the reigning monarchs for those occasions of state when they were required to address the assembled Lords. Around the throne were arranged the tiered seats reserved for the nobles, grouped according to the Ten Houses.

On this day, the normally austere throne was draped in purple cloth and garlands of gilded seaweed, in anticipation of the prince's arrival. The Lords' benches were packed, as were the public galleries above. The crowd was murmur-

ing expectantly, waiting for the royal procession to arrive.

There was a sudden flurry as a young Atlantean woman, dressed in the colors of House Taureus, her long reddish hair drifting about her delicately formed face like sea grass, made her way through the press of bodies. An older man, outfitted in the same house colors, stood up and waved as he called out her name:

"Tethys! Over here!"

The young girl smiled and waved back at her kinsman, kicking upward with her powerful legs and swimming over the heads of the assembly. With three strong strokes she settled into the seat beside him.

"Thank you for saving me a place, Cousin Tydeus! I wouldn't have wanted to miss this for all the salt in the ocean!"

Tydeus, Viscount of Charybdis, who was already losing his hair and had more of a belly than a merman under sixty had a right to, spluttered and looked highly embarrassed. "Tethys! One doesn't *swim* in the Congress of Lords!"

"Why not?"

"Because it's simply not *done*, young woman! The traditions of the Congress date back to long before the Cataclysm! People did not swim in the Congress *then*, so it is not done *now*!''

Tethys laughed, tossing her head back in such a way that everyone in the immediate vicinity looked in her direction. ''Cousin Tydeus, you really are too much! Must you always be so serious?''

Tydeus's fleshy cheeks darkened and he leaned forward, his voice becoming hard enough to crack an oyster. ''You forget your place, cousin! I may tolerate your girlish impudence at my dinner table, but this is another matter altogether! Your parents sent you to Atlantis so that I might improve your social graces and help you find a suitable mate! And until such time that you are not reliant upon my goodwill to provide you with food and shelter, you shall do as I say, is that understood?''

Tethys lowered her eyes and tucked her chin toward her collarbone, openly chagrined. ''Yes, cousin.''

Although she did not feel in the least remorseful, Tethys knew better than to anger her cousin any further. He meant well, but Tydeus was very stodgy and too conservative for her taste. She hoped she would find a suitor fairly soon, or her parents might very well make good on their threat to marry her off to him.

"Good! I didn't invite you here today simply out of the kindness of my heart! Although you have never been here before, as a member of the aristocracy, you have the right to vote. Today the prince plans to propose to make one of his lackeys—a low-born churl named Hiordis—a Lord of the Realm! While the prince has the power to nominate, it is up to the Congress to vote on the matter. I, and a few of my friends, plan to block Hiordis's election. Why, he is the son of a green-skinned Lemurian freedman! When the time comes for you to cast your vote, you are to raise your hand against his elevation. Have I made myself clear, Tethys?"

"Yes, cousin."

There was a commotion from the back of the building and the sound of a conch being blown. The gathered lords and ladies rose as one, and the commoners in the galleries stood on tiptoe and craned their necks for a better look as the prince made his entrance, accompanied by the Royal Guards.

Tethys tried to stifle a gasp of excitement as she leapt to her feet, eager for a glimpse of the fabled Namor. This was all so thrilling! It was times like this that made up for her having been placed under Tydeus's stewardship. After spending all those tiresome years in such a dismal outpost settlement as Aleutia, she was finally in Atlantis! And she was actually getting to see Namor himself—in the flesh!

However, it really wasn't her first time to do so. The prince had once paid her family's estate a brief visit, years ago, when Tethys was little more than an infant. Her mother, the Lady Merita, was a distant cousin of the royal family—but then, *every* Atlantean of noble blood was distantly related to the royal family in some way or another.

As Namor entered the Congress, Tethys saw the long purple cape he wore fastened about his broad shoulders and the green scale-mail trunks that had become his signature. In his right hand he held a trident scepter, the symbol of his office, and on his head rested the golden-spiked crown that had been worn by every ruler of Atlantis from time immemorial.

Tethys's dim childhood memories of the man had been of a towering, larger-than-life hero, both reassuring in his manner, yet frightening because of his physical differences. Part of her had been afraid that he might have shrunk over twenty years, dwindling in stature as she grew older. But seeing him now, she was surprised to find him still larger than life. If anything, he was even more impressive than she remembered. His pale skin and winged feet were still a bit disconcerting, especially to someone who had yet to lay eyes on an actual air-breather, but there was no denying that the Avenging Son was far from unattractive.

Namor held up his trident and the buzzing voices fell silent.

"Greetings, Lords and Ladies! It is my honor to address the Congress this day! I come before you to propose the name of Hiordis, son of Ruahatu the Lemurian, so that he may be made one of your number." Namor gestured with his free hand. A tall, rugged merman, dressed in the ceremonial armor of the Royal Guard, his right arm in a sling and left eye covered by a patch, stepped forward from the ranks of the honor guard. The only visible trace of Hiordis's Lemurian heritage was his green hair, which was plaited into a warrior's braid.

"Hiordis has served Atlantis valiantly during the recent war with our enemy, Attuma—going so far as to save my life at the cost of his own well-being! I propose to bestow upon him the title of Baron. What say you, the scions of the Ten Houses?''

Tydeus cleared his throat loudly and stood up. ''Your Highness—I object!''

Namor raised one upswept brow and fought to keep from smiling. ''You? Object? How novel, Viscount Tydeus.''

''Far be it from me to disparage the service that the brave Hiordis has done our homeland, Your Highness. Still—he is but a commoner! And not even one of full Atlantean parentage! His father was a Lemurian slave, taken in battle by your own grandfather! These things were not done in the days of our ancestors!''

Namor's smile faded and a stern, forbidding look came over his face. His voice was steady and firm, but the control could not disguise his evident displeasure. ''It is true that Hiordis's father, Ruahatu, was once a slave. But he was freed upon the death of my grandfather, and married the Lady Purana, Nereus's demi-daughter by one of his concubines. Hiordis was born long after his father had been given his freedom and made a citizen of Atlantis by my mother, Queen Fen. He is indirect blood-kin to the royal family. And you forget, Tydeus, that Ruahatu was a Lemurian king before he was a slave! I do not believe, good Lord, that you should speak so haughtily about the bloodlines of others.

"Three thousand years ago my ancestor, Karis the Just, allowed common-born Atlanteans and the sons of freed slaves to join the Congress. Many members of this august establishment owe their presence here today to my ancestor's break with Atlantean tradition! Your own branch of the family is hardly as noble as you would wish others to believe. I happen to know that your forefathers were selling shark meat in the streets during the reign of my great-great-grandfather, Tumalt XI."

"That's a lie!" Tydeus sputtered, as the gallery and the assembled Congress burst into laughter. "They were honest merchants!"

"Be that as it may, cousin," Namor chuckled, "shall we now put Hiordis's elevation to the vote? Whosoever is in favor of Hiordis, son of Ruahatu, being granted the title of Baron, do so by a show of hands."

Tydeus, still smarting from the dressing-down he'd received, blinked in disbelief as Tethys's hand shot up along with those of the others. "Tethys! What do you think you're doing?"

"Voting Hiordis into the Congress," she whispered.

"And whosoever is opposed—?" Namor prompted.

Fuming indignantly, Tydeus—along with a dozen others—raised his hand.

Namor smiled broadly and clapped Hiordis on the shoulder. "Let the record show that the son of Ruahatu the Lemurian was accepted into the Congress of Lords by an overwhelming majority! Congratulations, Lord Hiordis!"

As tradition demanded, the nobles were to file past the newly made Lord and introduce themselves. It was all Tydeus could do to keep from trembling with outrage as he stood in line beside his younger cousin.

"How dare you embarrass me in such a manner?" he hissed. "To vote against me in front of my friends and colleagues!"

"Come now, cousin," Tethys chided, trying her best to defuse his anger. "It's not as if my vote would have turned the tide! Besides, Hiordis is a hero! And hardly as base-born as you made him out to be!"

"Still, I will not speak as an equal to such a low-born hybrid!" Tydeus snarled. "And as for that half-breed bastard and his slur against our family—''

''But, Tydeus, what he said about our ancestors was *true*!''

''That is no excuse for holding me up to ridicule before the public gallery! The more I reflect on it, the less I like it! I will rot in the belly of the Leviathan before suffering such an insult!'' And with that, Tydeus gathered his cloak about himself and broke free of the reception line, heading in the direction of the exit.

Tethys watched him go, uncertain of the etiquette of the situation. Should she follow her kinsman or stay in line? Before she could determine the proper thing to do, she was surprised to find herself looking up into the face of the prince.

Namor smiled politely down at her, much the same way she remembered him doing when she was a child, shyly clutching her mother's skirt. ''I'm sorry—I'm afraid I don't recognize you, milady. Are you new to Atlantis?''

''Y-yes, Your Highness,'' she managed to squeak, her voice as high-pitched as a bottle-nose dolphin. ''My name is Tethys. My father is Lord Tarqis of Aleutia. I've only been here a few days . . .''

Namor's smile broadened. "Ah, yes! The last time I saw you, you were no bigger than a dogfish! How is your mother, the Lady Merita?"

"She is well and sends her warmest regards, Your Highness."

"Excellent! I'm glad to hear it! Lady Tethys, it is my pleasure to introduce you to Baron Hiordis. Hiordis, the Lady Tethys is a distant kinswoman of mine."

Hiordis, an exceptionally handsome young man made even more dashing by his eyepatch, bowed stiffly at the waist and lifted her powder-blue hand to his lips. "It is an honor, milady."

Tethys blushed so deeply that her cheeks turned indigo.

Namor, noticing the look on Tethys's face, worked to stifle a smile. "Now that you are here, you must come visit me in the palace, cousin! I would hear how fares Aleutia and my kinsmen in the Bering Sea. I am holding a banquet tomorrow in honor of Hiordis's elevation. Should I have my Chief Chamberlain add you to the guest list—?"

Tethys tried her best to regain her composure, smoothing the hair out of her face. "That's very kind of you, cousin—"

"Your Highness!"

Namor's smile disappeared quickly as he turned in the direction of the palace herald trying to make his way through the press of bodies and guards. There was an audible gasp as the assembly realized that a commoner was on the floor of the Congress.

"Sir! You must come at once to the palace!"

"What is it that is so important you would dare to come onto the floor of the Congress?" Namor demanded.

"Warlord Kreeg sent me, Your Highness! He has captured a human spy!"

There was a moment of stunned silence, then everyone began talking at once. Without saying another word, Namor quickly swam away, leaving the Royal Guards in his wake.

* * *

Kreeg and his captive were waiting in the throne room. Kreeg was big and burly, dressed in the armor of an Atlantean warlord, his forehead shaved into a widow's peak and his long hair braided into a single thick coil that hung down his back. Like most harpoon-masters, his face bore battle scars, and part of his left ear was missing. He wore a shark-tooth necklace and a belt woven from a captured fisherman's net was cinched about his waist.

Beside him was the captive, a human in a strangely constructed deep-sea diving suit that made him look like a bright yellow robot. The human's hands and feet were hobbled by lead weight-belts liberated from long-dead divers. The tanks strapped to his back hissed and bubbled noisily with each breath he took.

Also in attendance was Lord Seth, head general of the Royal Army. Seth, who was considerably younger than the veteran Kreeg, gave an audible sigh of relief as Namor swam into the audience chamber.

"What is the meaning of this?" Namor demanded, pointing at the diver.

"I have captured a spy, my prince, sent by the air-breathers to plot against us!" Kreeg announced, grinning nastily in the direction of the human. As a young warrior, Kreeg had been notorious for yanking deep-sea sports fishermen off excursion boats and into the water—even those strapped into chairs.

"I would have gutted him on the spot, except that Lord Seth insisted that the miserable wretch be brought before you!"

"And rightly so, Kreeg! No harm is to befall

those who traverse my realm—whether they are Atlantean or human!'' Namor peered through the plastic faceplate at the diver within the helmet. A pale-skinned male in his late twenties stared back out at him, eyes wide with terror.

Lord Seth lightly tapped the side of the diving helmet, which bore the emblem of a stylized tidal wave poised above a radiant sun. ''I recognize this symbol, Your Highness. It belongs to the Pan-Gaea Institute. They are scientists and scholars dedicated to the protection of the enviroment. This man is an enviromentalist!''

''He is an air-breather, therefore an enemy of Atlantis! I don't need a mewling, puddingheaded whelp to tell me who is or isn't my enemy!'' snarled Kreeg, thrusting his face into Seth's so that their noses all but touched.

''*Silence*!'' Namor thundered.

Kreeg and Seth stepped away, although the warlord's right hand still rested on the pommel of his war-trident.

''Seth is correct,'' Namor said, pointing in the direction of the cowering diver. ''This human is of no danger to the realm. See that he is safely returned to his research vessel.''

''Yes, my prince,'' Seth replied, escorting

the visibly relieved oceanographer from the royal presence.

"And as for *you*, Kreeg . . ." Namor turned to glower at the warlord. "Although I appreciate the fierceness of your loyalty—"

Kreeg lifted his head and met Namor's gaze, his eyes blazing with indignation. "My loyalty is to *Atlantis*. And Atlantis alone. I have no love of air-breathers—or those who would protect them!"

"You have served Atlantis well over the years, Kreeg. Therefore I shall ignore your tone of voice and overlook your insubordination. For *now*. You are excused from my presence, Warlord."

Kreeg swam off, muttering darkly under his breath. Just as he reached the door, Namor called out again.

"Kreeg!"

The warlord's shoulders went rigid as he slowly turned to face his ruler. Namor sat on the Throne of Neptune, his face unsmiling, the scepter resting across his knees.

"One last thought before you go—I would advise that you and your men leave the Pan-Gaea Institute's research vessel be. So speaks the Avenging Son."

Before Kreeg could respond, an Atlantean dressed in the finery of a high noble entered the throne room. He was tall, muscular, and completely hairless, except for a pencil-thin mustache, his scalp as smooth as that of a dolphin.

"Get away from me, churl!" he snapped at the royal page dogging his heels. "I don't have to be announced! I'm one of the royal family!"

"Ah. Cousin. I wondered when you would put in your appearance today."

Prince Byrrah, Namor's cousin and closest living blood relative, strode forward, sneering his usual welcome. "I've no need for your sarcasm, cousin. What's this I hear of you setting free a human spy?"

"There was no spy—only an oceanographer who wandered in the wrong direction, that is all."

"I suppose you let him live?"

"He was no threat. It's bad enough that the humans treat the seas as a handy dumping ground for their waste, without us slaughtering the few air-breathers interested in preserving the integrity of the oceans!"

"All air-breathers are a threat!"

Namor rolled his eyes and leaned back on

the throne. "*Must* we have this argument every day, Byrrah?"

"I will argue the point until you cast aside your foolishness and accept my words as truth! You once felt as I do—years ago you once waged a war on the air-breathers the likes of which they'd never seen!"

"I was but a youth then, as ignorant of the nature of the world above the waves as a hermit crab is of what lies beyond its shell! I have learned many things about surface-dwellers since then, cousin. Things you would do well to learn, if you would rule."

Byrrah blinked and looked somewhat abashed, as if his cousin had somehow read his mind. "M-my liege, I would not dare to—"

"Wouldn't you, cousin? You have lusted after the throne since we were boys, Byrrah. But there is more to being a ruler than sitting on a dais with a crown on your head and a scepter in your hand, yelling at those beneath you and ordering them to your fancy. Far more. If I allowed Kreeg to slay every human he laid his hands on, we'd soon find ourselves bombarded by explosive depth charges! We are a civilized kingdom, Byrrah—the oldest in existence! I do not wish to have creatures who were little more than upright apes when Atlantis sank beneath the waves dismiss us as barbarians.''

''Your Highness?''

Namor looked up from haranguing his cousin to focus on a timid-looking page standing in the doorway. ''Eh—? What is it, boy?''

''Lord Vashti sent me to, uh, remind you that you're due to appear at a presentation—?''

''See what I mean, cousin? The affairs of state are endless! Will you accompany me, Byrrah?''

''No. I have—business—I must attend to elsewhere.''

''Very well. I shall see you at dinner, then. Come, boy—lead me to whatever function it is that cannot start until I grace it with my attention.''

* * *

Byrrah stood and watched his cousin leave the throne room, rage and envy burning inside him like the heart of a drowned volcano. It wasn't fair that a pink-skinned freak such as Namor should sit on the throne! By all rights, it should have been his.

In the beginning it was Byrrah who had been groomed to succeed the old king. His father was the old man's son by his head concubine, which normally precluded ascension to the throne. But Nereus's queen, Amphitrite, had borne him only daughters—the Princesses Fen and Zorya. Even when Fen produced Namor, Byrrah had not seen it as a threat to his destiny. After all, Fen's child was both a half-breed and illegitimate.

But Prince Nereus had been counselled by the temple priests that the hybrid was a champion sent by the god Poseidon, and when the wings on his ankles sprouted, the old fool had taken it as a divine sign and named Namor the Heir Apparent.

Even after he had been demoted to a mere prince of the realm, Byrrah still held on to his dreams of glory. Once Namor discovered the surface world—earning the ludicrous title of ''Sub-Mariner'' from its denizens—he began to neglect his kingdom.

First he spent his time warring against the air-breathers by sinking their ships and destroying their fishing nets. Then he became enamored of one of their females and actually helped battle one kind of air-breather in particular, a group calling themselves ''the Axis,'' or somesuch, as if the creatures could actually be told apart! Then, after the war between the surface-dwellers was over, Namor simply disappeared.

Namor was assumed dead, although Nereus refused to make it official. When the old king finally died, Fen served as regent, with Byrrah next in the line of succession. Queen Fen's reign was short, compared to that of her father's, and many claimed she died of a broken heart, mourning the loss of her prodigal son. And just as Byrrah was about to claim that which was rightfully his, the pale-skinned freak swam back into Atlantis. No doubt the flat-headed squid had spent the years away from his homeland dallying with human females.

"A gold piece for your thoughts, good prince."

Byrrah, startled, turned to look at the speaker. "Ah, Kreeg. I didn't notice you standing there in the shadows."

"There is much to be learned in the shadows, my prince. Much indeed."

Byrrah shrugged. "What do you want?"

"I bring you a message from our benefactor. He asks that we meet with him this night in the appointed place. He wants to know if you are ready to make your move."

Byrrah looked about uneasily. "Tell him I'll be there. I can't wait any longer. The time to return Atlantis to her former glory is finally at hand.''

* * *

The meeting with Byrrah and Kreeg's benefactor was to take place in the secluded grotto of an underground cave, miles beyond the walls of Atlantis. When Byrrah arrived, he found a second figure awaiting him in the shadows with Kreeg: Tydeus, the Viscount Charybdis.

As Byrrah approached, Kreeg hefted his harpoon and held it menacingly, relaxing only when he recognized his co-conspirator. ''What kept you?'' he snarled.

''Don't use that tone with me, Kreeg!'' Byrrah replied testily. ''I came as soon as I could without being noticed! The royal palace is all aflutter with preparations for tomorrow's banquet.''

''In honor of that half-breed upstart Hiordis!'' Tydeus snorted derisively. ''Namor's disregard for Atlantean tradition is bringing this kingdom to its ruination!''

Kreeg nodded his head. ''He has allowed himself to be swayed by the surface-dwellers. He refuses to war against them, even though they continue to defile our homeland with their garbage, dragnets, and oil spills! For all his supposed strength, he is weak as a child!"

"Where is our benefactor? I thought he would he here by now," Byrrah said, looking about anxiously.

"Relax, gentlemen. You need wait no further."

Tydeus yelped in alarm as the shadows that had pooled in the deepest corner of the cave now stepped forward. Kreeg tightened his grip on the haft of his harpoon. Byrrah tried to keep the alarm from registering on his face, but didn't quite succeed.

Even to his fellow surface-dwellers, Victor Von Doom was an unnerving sight. The only part of his anatomy not completely sealed away behind body armor were his eyes—and they were indeed fearsome to behold. Byrrah had seen kindlier moray eels. He wondered how it was that Kreeg had been able to make contact with Doom in the first place, but held his tongue. It didn't do to ask questions of either man—and he was not about to question Doom's interest in participating in their little conspiracy.

"H-how long have you been standing there?"

"Long enough," replied Dr. Doom. "I trust

you have decided to take action or you would not be here."

The three Atlanteans exchanged glances, but it was Byrrah who spoke. "Yes. It is time. We can no longer tolerate Namor as our ruler."

"*Excellent.*" Although there was no way they could be sure, Von Doom seemed to be smiling from behind his cast-iron mask. He produced a small vial the size and shape of a perfume bottle, holding it up between his metallic thumb and forefinger so the others might see.

"I took the sample of Namor's tissue Kreeg provided, and used it as the matrix for a genetically engineered virus designed to affect the Sub-Mariner's hybrid immune system." Byrrah wondered how Kreeg managed the feat—probably bribed the Royal Physician. Or even threatened him; that would be more in character for the warlord.

Doom continued, "The virus is colorless, odorless, tasteless. Once ingested by the Sub-Mariner, it will begin its work almost immediately—rendering him as weak as a newborn baby within a matter of days. Which should give you, Prince Byrrah, ample opportunity to step in and take control."

Byrrah frowned as he took the proffered

vial. "What if he tries to escape to the surface? He has many dangerous allies he can call upon for help." Byrrah knew that Namor had associated with many of the surface world's so-called super heroes over the years, including the Avengers, the Defenders, and the Fantastic Four.

"Worry not, Prince Byrrah," Doom said. "The virus also impedes his ability to breathe air. While the membranes that allow him to extract oxygen from water remain intact, his lungs will be rendered incapable of breathing out of water. Should he choose to take refuge on the surface, he will asphyxiate within minutes."

This placated Byrrah to some degree, but he was still worried. "How are we to secrete this into Namor's food or drink? Everything he imbibes must first go through the Royal Taster."

"The beauty of this virus, my good prince, is that it can affect only one person—and that is Namor! Full-blooded Atlanteans will remain untouched, I assure you."

Tydeus smiled. "Allow me, my prince. I have an idea as to how we can best make sure the half-breed drinks his fill."

* * *

Namor stood in the receiving line with Hiordis, shaking hands and exchanging pleasantries as the guests filed into the banquet hall. He lifted an eyebrow as he caught a glimpse of Tethys standing nearby, and nudged Hiordis.

"It seems that you are indeed in luck, cousin! The Lady Tethys has arrived!"

Hiordis straightened his shoulders and somehow managed to stand a little taller than before.

"Ah, Lady Tethys!" Namor smiled warmly. "How good of you to come! And what is this you're carrying—?"

Tethys held up a bottle the color of sapphire. "It is a gift, Your Highness, from my cousin, Tydeus. He wishes to apologize for his outburst of the other day. It is vintage *klerys*."

"*Klerys*, eh?" Namor took the bottle from Tethys and eyed it appreciatively. The drink was a liqueur made from fermented orca milk, and was prized for both its potency and rarity. "Tell your cousin when you next see him I am most pleased. Come, my dear—sit at our table! I would hear of my kinsfolk in the Bering Sea, and I'm certain Baron Hiordis would find what you have to say most interesting as well."

* * *

Namor was pleased by how quickly Hiordis and Tethys were responding to one another. Although his own love life was often far from happy, he delighted in playing matchmaker with his subjects every now and again. Hiordis was young, brave, and handsome, with a promising future, although he did suffer, as did Namor himself, from the stigma of mixed blood. Tethys was quite lovely, vivacious, and intelligent, yet her branch of the family was far from prosperous. It would not do to have such a delightful girl married off to a pompous old walrus like Tydeus.

Namor lifted the jewel-encrusted conch shell that served as his goblet to his lips, savoring the heady richness of fermented orca milk. Oh, well. Tydeus might be a barnacle-encrusted reactionary, but at least he knew his *klerys*.

* * *

Namor awoke the next day feeling sluggish, but dismissed it out of hand. No doubt he'd had a little too much *klerys* the night before. Vashti commented on his prince's appearance and offered to call for the Royal Physician, but Namor shook his head.

''I have no need for the surgeon's lamprey, Vashti. I merely overindulged at the banquet, that is all. You know how fond I am of jellied octopus and pickled moray. I'll be fine come the afternoon. Besides, I'm to review the Seventh Regiment today.''

Namor was mildly surprised to find Byrrah waiting to accompany him in the courtyard. ''I was not aware that you were interested in the state of the army, cousin.''

''I am interested in all things that involve Atlantis's welfare, Namor. But if you wish me to remain in the city—''

''No, by all means, you are welcome to join my retinue. I did not mean it as an insult. I was merely—surprised, that's all.''

The Seventh Regiment was stationed at the farthest reaches of Atlantis's borders, and was trained to handle incursions from the barbarian tribes that harried the various outposts. Namor was there to inspect the troops and award military honors to some for their recent bravery in battle. As tumultuous as Atlantis's days had been before the Great Cataclysm, they were nothing compared to the constant danger it endured under the sea.

As Namor took his place of honor on the reviewing stand, he felt an uncharacteristic weakness in his knees, but quickly pushed it out of his mind. Throughout his life he had enjoyed excellent health and was unaccustomed to anything but the mildest discomfort. Within an hour's time, however, his insides began to twist into painful knots. One moment he was standing on the podium, watching the harpoon-masters undergo their defensive drill, the next he was on his knees, his body wreaked with violent spasms of heat and cold. He was vaguely aware of his cousin kneeling beside him, asking him if he was ill.

Lord Seth hurried forward. "My prince! What is wrong—? Should I summon the camp physician?"

Byrrah shook his head as he cradled his ailing kinsman to him. "What good would your surgeon be to him? Are any of your soldiers of human and Atlantean parentage? No, he must be tended to by the Royal Physician—one familiar with his unique metabolism. He is obviously too sick to make the trip back to Atlantis! Luckily, I have an estate not too far from here. Warlord Kreeg has been good enough to volunteer his aid in transporting the prince. I'll see to it that he's made comfortable until the Royal Physician arrives."

Seth eyed Kreeg uncertainly but did not dare

argue with Byrrah. After all, he was the prince's blood relative.

* * *

Byrrah had inherited his estate from his mother's side of the family. It had once been the seat of their power, until the barbarian reavers forced them to relocate within Atlantis's sheltering walls. Now it served Byrrah as a hunting lodge—and killing floor.

Namor was placed in one of the guest rooms, where he lay—feverish and fading in and out of consciousness—on a bed of old seaweed. Byrrah was quick to dismiss the servants from the sickroom and lock the door behind them.

"It's working just like he said it would," Kreeg muttered in awe, fingering his beard as he watched Namor moan. "Von Doom is a genius! Too bad he's a surface-dweller."

"Of course it's working," Byrrah replied. "I might not know much about the surface world, but I know enough not to doubt Doom's word."

"But what of the others? Seth is certain to notify Vashti of the prince's predicament. He'll bring the Royal Physician with him—"

"And what can the old cod do? Let him poke and prod and palpitate to his heart's content! Doctor Aegus has neither the knowledge nor the ability to reverse the course of the virus.'' Byrrah leaned over his cousin's sickbed, grinning down at him. ''Too bad you will die without issue, cousin.''

Namor's eyes opened at the sound of his kinsman's voice, but did not seem to focus.

''You were foolish to ignore the royal harem for the charms of the late, unlamented Ladies Dorma and Marrina. But fear not—I will be proud to take up the trident and the crown as your successor! The House of Poseidon shall continue. And, under my reign, it will rise triumphant over the foolish air-breathers who would dare to abuse us!''

''B-Byrrah? You did this to me?'' Namor whispered.

''Aye. Although I cannot take full credit for the sickness that is destroying you. You must thank Tydeus's poisoned *klerys* for that.''

''Traitor! *Usurper*!'' snarled Namor, struggling to sit up.

''Temper-temper, cousin! You don't want to overexert yourself!''

''You'll pay for this treachery, Byrrah! By our grandfather's bones, I swear it!''

''And how do you intend to make good on

your oath, eh?'' sneered Byrrah. He emitted a single, high-pitched squeak of terror as Namor's right hand darted forward, clamping itself tightly about his throat. Grim-faced and shivering, Namor leveraged himself out of bed without loosening his grip on his cousin.

"Even at death's portal, the Sub-Mariner is still powerful enough to treat you like the flotsam you are!"

"Kreeg! *Do* something!" Byrrah gasped.

The warlord hefted his harpoon, reversing it so that the shaft struck Namor on the back of the head. Namor staggered and dropped Byrrah, who lay cowering on the floor, clutching at his bruised gills.

Namor turned to face Kreeg, struggling to focus through the raging fever that clouded his eyes and threatened to pull him downward into darkness. "I should have known—Byrrah would have turned—to the likes of you—"

"And it shall be the likes of me that will skewer your half-breed heart, 'Sub-Mariner'," sneered Kreeg, keeping Namor at arm's length by jabbing him with the point of his harpoon. "I'll chop you up for chum and feed you to the sharks!"

"Kreeg, you bloody-minded fool!" Byrrah

yelled. "No! There can't be any marks on the body! We can't afford a coroner's inquest, or anything that might endanger my succession!"

"All well and good for you to say, seeing how you're the one that provoked him," Kreeg retorted.

* * *

For all his bravado, Namor's strength began to ebb. His brief burst of anger had driven him to his feet, but now it was fading. He wished it wasn't so hard to think. Where was Vashti? Vashti could help him think better. Vashti would tell him what was wrong. He needed help. Help. He had to go get help. Before it was too late. Too late for him. Too late for Atlantis.

Summoning his remaining strength, Namor smashed the side of his hand against Kreeg's harpoon, splintering the shaft, and shot past the surprised warlord, punching his way through the crumbling wall as if it were made of toy blocks.

"Don't just stand there!" Byrrah shouted. "He's getting away!"

Kreeg's reply was to grab Byrrah by the front of his tunic.

"What are you doing?!? Unhand me! You dare touch the Royal Person—?!?"

Kreeg thrust his scarred face into Byrrah's

so that their noses were touching. "Shut up! You started this, and I'll be damned if you're not going to be there when it ends!"

The voices of the traitors faded as Namor pushed himself onward. His thoughts dwindled to simple commands: *Swim. Swim faster. Have to get away. Have to get help.*

Part of him was vaguely aware that his swimming prowess had been affected by whatever it was that was making him sick. Normally, he could swim rings around the fleetest of dolphins—but this was not a normal day. He could feel his strength dwindling quickly, but he continued to press onward. He could not fail. His life and kingdom were at stake.

Namor began heading toward the surface, the one place he knew his enemies could not follow.

* * *

"Kreeg! Stop him! He's heading for the surface!"

"I can *see* that, you yammering fool!" the warlord grunted. "Shoot him!"

The inside of Byrrah's mouth grew bitter. "But how will we explain it to the others?"

"We'll think of something later! If we don't stop him now, fish will nibble away our faces while our heads rot on pikes!''

Kreeg was right. There was no other way. Even blood as royal as his own would not protect him from the penalty meted out to those found guilty of high treason. Byrrah lifted his harpoon gun and aimed it in the direction of his fleeing cousin.

As he sighted down the barrel, he was amazed at how severely the virus had affected his kinsman. He'd never seen Namor move so sluggishly before. Ever since childhood, his younger cousin had always been a prodigious physical specimen: faster, stronger, and more agile than the kindgom's greatest athletes.

As his finger tightened on the trigger, he remembered the years he had spent in the frigid water of the Arctic. For several centuries Atlantis had been forced by its enemies to relocate from its original site to the Bering Sea. As a boy, he'd delighted in playing cruel pranks on the Inuit natives who ranged the ice floes: overturning their kayaks, stealing their catches, frightening them by bursting through the ice while they hunted for seals.

His parents had insisted that he take his younger cousin with him on these expeditions, as they wished their son to become close to the new Heir Apparent. Byrrah couldn't have been more than eleven or twelve at the time, which would have made Namor six. Needless to say, he had resented Namor's presence a great deal.

While they were swimming along, looking for dangling fishing lines to yank on, Byrrah found himself screaming in agony. He had been mistaken for a seal by a hunter on the surface armed with a harpoon. The sight of the wicked whalebone barb protruding through his thigh had caused Byrrah to go into shock. The seal-hunter began reeling in the line attached to the harpoon, so he could drag his catch onto the ice and club out its brains.

It was Namor who had possessed the presence of mind to use his shark-tooth knife to cut the harpoon line and hurry Byrrah back to their parents for help. It was the first time his cousin had saved his life and the first time he'd made Byrrah look a weakling.

Now he had the chance to change all that, now and forever. All he had to do was pull the trigger—

"You missed him! You *deliberately* missed him!" Kreeg thundered.

Byrrah blinked, not even aware that he'd fired the harpoon gun. His thigh ached with a phantom pain six decades gone. "It doesn't matter. He's as good as dead once he reaches the surface. Remember what Von Doom said? He can no longer survive on the surface."

* * *

The surface of the ocean parted like a caul and Namor, the Sub-Mariner, shot into the sky like a leaping dolphin, only to be hurled back into the crashing waves by hurricane-force winds. The sky was full of angry, roiling clouds the color of a ripe bruise. Mustering what remained of his strength, Namor tried to break free of the ocean's hold once more, the wings on his ankles beating so fiercely it felt as if they would yank themselves free. He managed to climb fifty feet into the storm-laden sky before the winds drove him into the sea a final time.

* * *

He was lying face down, the water covering his head. He was vaguely aware of being on a beach, because he could feel the sand under his body. He could hear gulls squabbling nearby, fighting over something the storm had washed up. Perhaps him.

He had to find help. But first he had to figure out where he was. Too bad he didn't have the strength to roll over on his back and look at the sky.

Something nudged him sharply in the ribs, and for a heartbeat he felt a surge of fear. Had Byrrah and Kreeg found him? Or was a curious shark prodding him to make sure he was dead before taking a bite? No. The water was too shallow for that. Besides, a shark would hardly care if he was dead or not.

He was lying on a beach in less than a foot of surf, of that he was certain. Painfully bright light struck his eyes as he was rolled onto his back and the gulls' screams grew louder. He could barely make out what looked to be a human face peering down at him. Namor reached out and tried to grip his savior's arm. It was important that he understand who he was. What was wrong with him. What was at stake.

But all that came out of his mouth was: "Help—Susan—"

Then he realized he couldn't breathe anymore.

CHAPTER 2

THE NATURE
OF THINGS

New York, New York is a helluva town, as the song goes. Among the many wonderful sights to be found in the city that never sleeps (according, at least, to another song) is Four Freedom's Plaza, home of the world's greatest heroes, the Fantastic Four.

From the outside, the Plaza looks no more or less strange than other cliff dwellings of the rich and famous. Like many of New York's most famous structures, it has a distinctive style. The Flatiron has its odd shape, the Empire State Building has its spire, the Citicorp Building its slanted roof, the *Daily Bugle* building the newspaper's name emblazoned on its roof; so, too, does Four Freedom's Plaza have its special quirk, in this case the stylized numeral 4 etched into the top of each of the building's four sides. But inside—well, that's a different matter altogether.

* * *

Susan Richards, better known to the world as the Invisible Woman, lowered her protective goggles and squinted through the three-foot-thick plasti-form window into the room beyond the control booth. "I don't know, Reed—are you sure this is safe?"

Her husband shrugged. Without moving from his seat, he reached for a calibration tool on the other side of the room, picked it up, and consulted the readout blinking on its screen. Reed Richards was known and respected the world over as one of the greatest scientific geniuses alive. That, and the fact that he was a super-powered adventurer capable of stretching his body like a rubber band, was the reason he was called Mr. Fantastic.

"Science is not without its hazards, Sue. You know that as well as I do. There is a chance that the feedback from the cosmic-ray inversion chamber might generate an explosion. That's why I asked you to be present. Should such a crisis arise, I'll need you to use your force field to help contain the blast.'' Reed twisted his head completely around on his neck so that he was looking directly at his wife. ''Sue—please put your safety goggles back on! It's better to be safe than sorry in situations like this.''

Sue sighed, sliding the eyewear back into place. ''Would it be all right if I went into the inversion chamber to wish Ben good luck one last time?''

Richards smiled, exposing the loving husband and loyal friend that lurked beneath the exterior of scientific genius and team leader. ''I don't see what harm it can do. A positive emotional and mental state may very well be instrumental to the outcome of the experiment.''

Sue opened the door that led from the observation booth to the cosmic-ray inversion chamber. The room was the size of an airplane hangar, filled to the rafters with esoteric machinery that no one but her husband and two Nobel physicists could comprehend. Seated in the middle of the vast jumble of super-scientific hardware, strapped to a padded armature, was something that resembled a fearsome gargoyle from ancient history.

As broad as it was tall, the creature was

shaped like a man. Instead of skin, however, the outside of its hairless body was covered by thousands of scales that, on closer examination, resembled interlocking orange-colored cobblestones. With a lipless mouth, beetling brow, and eight fingers and toes, it was indeed a beast capable of inspiring nightmares.

"Ben—are you comfortable? Is there anything I can get you?"

Benjamin Grimm—known to millions as the Thing—smiled and shook his head as best he could, considering his position. "Naw, I don't think so, Suzie. Although if I'd known yer egghead of a hubby was gonna take this long, I'd'a brought me a magazine to pass the time."

"Reed thinks that if he can sustain the inversion process just a little longer this time, he might fully reverse the effects of the cosmic radiation. I've never seen him so sure of anything before."

"I hope he's right, Suzie. I hope Reed can change me back to the way I used to be. Otherwise, when I retire I'm gonna have to move to Paris and haunt Notre Dame."

Sue bit her lip. Despite the jocular tone, Ben was scared. She could tell. But then, how many times had Reed tried to change Ben back to his human form and failed? It was difficult not to be jaded.

Reed's voice came over the intercom, sounding like that of NASA Control. "I'm about to start the countdown. Sue, I'll need you back in the observation booth . . ."

"Coming." She leaned forward and quickly pecked Ben on the cheek. It was like kissing pavement. "Good luck," she whispered. "I'm praying for you."

"Thanks, Suzie."

* * *

Ben Grimm watched Sue exit the chamber, then heard the voice of her husband crackling over the speakers: "Hold tight, old friend."

Yeah, sure, Stretch, Ben thought, *like I could do anything else.*

The Thing took a deep breath, readying himself for the pain he knew would soon be upon him. "Here goes nothin'!"

The machinery that filled the inversion chamber began to hum like a swarm of angry bees, the pitch growing higher until the very air vibrated like a tuning fork. Reed had explained the process to him earlier—or at least had tried to. Scientific gobbledygook aside, they were trying to reverse the process that had taken Benjamin Grimm, top-notch test pilot, and turned him into the orange-skinned behemoth called the Thing. It was by no means the first time he'd undergone such experiments in hopes of reclaiming his lost humanity. But he prayed this would be the one that worked.

The first jolt slammed into him like a freight car. Although he knew it was coming, it still didn't help. His muscles went rigid, as if they had turned to stone like his skin. His back arched and he closed his eyes as the pain slammed through his body, penetrating every cell. It was almost as bad as that first time, back in the rocket, when he and the others had been bombarded by the strange cosmic rays that had given them their powers. It felt as if he were being taken apart, molecule by molecule, his body reshaped by invisible hands. And just when he was convinced the pain was as bad as it could get, some joker reached inside him and made it even worse.

The smell of ozone and the sizzling pop of circuits frying made him open his eyes in time to see smoke and flames spurt from one of Reed's myriad framistats. *Overload*, he thought. *Figgers*.

The explosion seemed almost anticlimactic.

* * *

"Ben? Ben, are you all right? For the love of God, answer me, man!" Reed's neck zig-zagged crazily through the tangle of wrecked machinery and loosened masonry. The smell of burning circuitry filled the air. "Johnny! Get in here! I need your help in containing these electrical fires!"

Johnny Storm, Susan's younger brother, hurried into the room. "I read you loud and clear, leader-man. *Flame on!*" His right arm suddenly burst into flame, the fire licking at his body without harming his clothes or his flesh. "I'll absorb the flames, brother-in-law—you try and find the big galoot!"

Reed sent his neck limbo-ing under a fallen ceiling beam, then arcing over a computer bank that had collapsed onto its side during the explosion. Where was Ben? Sue had used her force field powers to protect the inversion chamber's exterior wall, so he was certain Ben couldn't have been blown out the side of the building like last time. He was still paying off the bills for the damage done during that particular experiment.

"Ben! Can you hear me—are you hurt?"

Susan Richards faded into sight beside her husband. "I did my best to throw a force bubble around him just before the equipment blew. I only hope I wasn't too late!"

There was a loud groan and the sound of movement from behind a nearby pile of wreckage. Sue reached out with her mind and, using the powers given her by the same cosmic rays that had transformed the others, shifted the rubble so that they could reach their friend. But what they saw caused them to freeze in their tracks.

Ben Grimm sat up and held his temples gingerly between his hands. "Ohhh—did anyone get th' number o' that bus?"

Johnny hurried over to join them, extinguishing his flame. "I took care of the fires. What about Ben? Is he—holy smoke!"

"Ya wanna hold it down, hot stuff? I got me th' mother of all migraines here!" Ben grimaced. "You three can stop yer squawkin'—I'm still in one piece!"

"B-Ben, that's not all you are!" Sue stammered.

"Whaddaya mean? Hey—why are you guys

lookin' at me like that—?'' Then he realized what was wrong. He was cold. And he itched. In the years since his skin had been replaced by the super-tough orange scales that covered his body, he had lost most of his sense of touch. He could feel only the most severe extremes of pain and temperature. It was like being trapped in a walking sensory deprivation chamber. But now he could feel the cold on his skin.

His *skin*!

Almost not daring to look, for fear of disappointment, Ben glanced down at his body. Instead of a vast expanse of craggy orange brick, he found himself staring at healthy pink flesh. His hands went to his head and he grinned from ear to ear, tears brimming in his eyes.

''Hair! I got hair again!''

He lowered his hands and held them out in front of him, splaying his fingers as far as they could go. ''And fingers! Look, Suzie! I got ten of 'em again! Just like when I was born into this lousy, crummy, stinkin', *beautiful* world!''

''Yes, Ben. I see them,'' Sue said, smiling through her tears.

''You did it, Reed! You did it! I'm cured!'' Ben laughed, lurching to his feet. He took a step forward to embrace his friend, then grabbed the waistband of his blue trunks to keep them from falling down around his ankles. "Whoops! I don't wanna repay your help by moonin' everyone!"

Johnny grinned and slapped Ben on the shoulder. "Way to go, old timer!"

"I hate to interrupt your moment of glory, Ben," Reed said as he reeled the rest of his body into the room. "But before we go any further, I need to run a few diagnostic tests on you, just to be on the safe side—"

"What's to be safe about, High Pockets? I'm Ben Grimm again—arrh!" Ben's smiling, happy face suddenly contorted into a mask of pain as he clutched his abdomen.

"Ben!" Sue reached out to him as he fell to his knees. "Ben—what is it!?!"

He tried to answer, but all that came out was a strangled groan. Sue turned to her husband, hoping he could tell her that what they all knew was happening wasn't really happening. Mr. Fantastic's face was somber as his oldest friend writhed on the floor.

"It's what I was afraid of. There simply wasn't enough time before the circuitry blew. The transformation was not permanent. He's turning back into the Thing.''

As his teammates watched, powerless to help, Ben Grimm's body began to grow, the muscles and bones becoming denser and denser. His hands expanded in diameter, the ring finger absorbing the pinkie. His skin darkened and became first leathery and wrinkled, like that of an elephant, then grew into the familiar, bricklike orange armor plating. The transformed Ben Grimm staggered to his feet, screaming at the top of his lungs.

''No! Not again!''

He raised one pile-driver fist and struck out. The entire building shook as the wall separating the inversion chamber and the control room disappeared. On the street outside Four Freedom's Plaza car alarms went off.

''Ben! Control yourself! You'll bring the whole building down around our ears!'' Reed yelled, wrapping himself around the Thing like a python, pinning his arms to his side.

''It ain't fair! What'd I ever do to deserve bein' turned into a freakin' monster? What!?!''

''Ben—calm down! I know you're disappointed—believe me, we all are! But this isn't how to deal with it!''

''Get offa me!''

Reed stretched his neck across the room to his wife. "Sue!"

Sue nodded quickly in response, knowing instinctively what to do. Seeing that his wife understood, Mr. Fantastic retracted his body, his limbs springing outward like a jack-in-the-box being opened. At the exact same moment, the Invisible Woman projected a force bubble about the Thing's head. Although invisible, the force field was far from intangible. It effectively cut off the Thing's oxygen supply.

Ben clawed at his throat, his blue eyes bulging from their sockets, then collapsed like the proverbial ton of bricks, shaking the entire room. Sue dissolved the force bubble the moment he lost consciousness.

Reed knelt beside his fallen friend, absent mindedly massaging the muscles in his shoulders. He might have the elasticity of rubber, but trying to contain the Thing was hardly a cakewalk. "I blame myself for this," he sighed. "Each time I succeed in reversing the transformation—but only for a short time. I'm beginning to think that instead of helping him, I'm only tormenting him—holding out a hope for an impossible 'cure.'"

Sue stood by her husband, gently stroking

the gray at his temples. "Reed—you're only doing the best that you can. You're his friend.
You're helping him the only way you know
how . . ."

"It's my fault that he's like this, Sue! If I
hadn't talked him into piloting the rocket ship,
he'd never have been subjected to the cosmic
rays that turned him into the Thing in the first
place!"

"Reed, no one blames you for what happened—certainly not Ben!"

"Sis is right, Reed," Johnny said, putting a
reassuring hand on his brother-in-law's shoulder.
"You shouldn't blame yourself."

"You lissen to the squirt, Stretch," rasped
the Thing, sitting up. "He might be a no-nothin'
pipsqueak, but he's right on that account."

"Ben—are you all right?" Reed asked.

"Yeah. Naw. Mebbe. I feel like a real putz,
in any case." He rubbed the back of his head as
he surveyed the wreckage of what was once the
cosmic-ray inversion chamber. "Aw, man—did
I do alla that?"

"Not all of it. Some of it blew up, remember?"

"Well, that's somethin'. I still feel like a
first-class heel. After all you done tryin' to help

me, I go an' try to tear the damn building down around our ears!''

Sue tried to hug the Thing, but her arms didn't even make it halfway around his middle. ''It's okay, Ben! It's not your fault! We understand.''

Ben gently pulled her away from him. ''It's sweet of you to say so, Suzie. The trouble is, I don't understand. Look—I gotta have some time to think about what's going on with my life, y'know? I need to take stock of myself.''

Reed frowned with concern. ''Are you sure you're okay, Ben?''

''All I'm sure of right now, High Pockets, is that I ain't fit company for man nor beast. I'll let you know if I'll be out overnight, okay?''

With that, the Thing turned his orange back on his friends and lumbered from the room. Sue pressed herself against her husband, who slipped his arm around her waist a few times.

''Reed—I'm really worried about Ben.''

''I know. And I share your concern. We keep forgetting that he's not solid brick. Despite all his bluster and joking around, there's a sensitive, intelligent, and frustrated man beneath that rough orange exterior. I only hope that he doesn't allow its weight to crush the soul inside.''

* * *

Ben Grimm opened the door to his closet and took out his camel-hair coat and battered fedora. He'd had the coat specially made a few years ago—it had set him back a few bucks, but it was worth it. With shoulders wide enough to accommodate a refrigerator and huge buttons designed for his large, often clumsy fingers, it reached his knees and was cut to mask his four hundred-plus pounds, so he could walk amongst the city's streets without calling undue attention to himself. Not that native New Yorkers would have batted an eye. It was the tourists he had to watch out for. Most of them were well-meaning fans, wanting an autograph or a chance to be photographed in the company of a ''real-live super hero.'' Others, however, were far from benign. He'd learned early in his career that some people are drawn to those with tough-guy reputations. These were the jokers who always wanted to pick fights or mouth off, knowing he wouldn't dare lift a hand for fear of looking bad in the press. And then there were the real nutcases. The ones who wanted to see if the Thing really was as big and bad as they said. They were the ones who carried guns or knives or baseball bats. *Those* kind of fans he could live without—especially the way he was feeling right now.

He pulled the fedora down low over his face, the brim resting on the thick shelf that served as his brow, as he stepped into the elevator that would take him to the secret exit. The paparazzi and other professional celebrity-watchers kept constant vigil at the main entrance of Four Freedom's Plaza. He had no desire to deal with those vultures.

Midtown Manhattan was as busy as ever when he stepped out of the nondescript doorway that opened onto the side street next to the Plaza. He shook his head in disgust. He still couldn't get used to the name. After so many years in the Baxter Building, their new headquarters sounded like a cross between the federal district court building and Trump Tower. Ben fell into pace with the surging tide of businesspeople, tourists, and garden-variety New Yorkers, doing his best not to call attention to himself by keeping his head lowered and his hands in his pockets.

He really needed to mull things over. Not that he ever got much time alone to himself. Over the years it seemed as if his life had devolved into a series of disasters, apocalypses, and catastrophes, with the odd Armageddon thrown in. Hell, every time he turned around it seemed as if some two-bit super-villain with an attitude was trying to take over the world, or alter the flow of time, or sell the planet to brain-sucking space-demons from Dimension X. Lately, he'd begun to feel nostalgic for the old days when they dealt with plain old criminals, like Paste Pot Pete. Things were simpler then. No cosmos-eating mega-aliens like Galactus or other such malarkey.

Yeah, it seemed like his life had turned into one long, extended fight scene, where he was constantly hammering the pea soup out of some scuzz-bucket. In the years since his transformation into the Thing, Ben had allowed circumstances to dictate the pattern of his life. He kept telling himself that marriage, children, happiness, retirement—all the things a man looks forward to and plans for—would have to wait until he was cured. But he could no longer delude himself. There was no cure.

So what now? Was he destined to spend the rest of his days as the bachelor member of the Fantastic Four, beating the tar out of every bad guy from Annihilus to Zontar, the Thing from

Venus? His mama raised him to deal responsibly with the hand life dealt him—but she could never have foreseen her pride-and-joy being mutated into a walking pile of orange bricks. And lately he had begun to wonder if the cosmic rays that had made him the Thing might not have altered him in more ways than even Reed imagined. What if he lived to be a hundred? Two hundred? What if he *couldn't* grow old? Never had the possibility of immortality been so unwelcome.

As he rounded the corner onto Sixth Avenue, heading for the Rockefeller Center subway station, he accidently collided with an elderly woman, sending her packages flying.

"Geez, I'm sorry, ma'am," he apologized, bending to retrieve a parcel. "Here, let me help you—"

The old woman smiled, apparently reassured by Ben's voice. "Thank you, young man. That's quite gentlemanly of you—" Her voice died away.

Hands the size of catcher's mitts, covered by a strange orange material, jutted from the cuffs of the stranger's coat sleeves. The hands—if that's what they were—didn't seem to have the right number of fingers. Too shocked to do more than gasp, she lifted her eyes to the face all but hidden by the fedora's shadow. It was not in the least human—except for the eyes. The eyes were robin's egg blue and were all too painfully aware of what was going through her head.

"You poor thing," was all she could think to say.

* * *

He tried not to feel angry as he hurried into the subway. At least the old lady didn't scream or faint or drop dead from a heart attack. He should count his lucky stars for that at least. He'd inspired more than his fair share of shock, fear, and disgust over the years. He'd learned how to deal with that crap. It was the pity that still got him.

You poor thing.

"Thing."

That's what he was, all right. A thing. The Thing.

As he stood on the platform, waiting for the train, he wondered what had possessed him to pick that name. Granted, they'd all made rather obvious choices when they picked their "stage names" back then. Invisible Girl. Human Torch. The Thing. Except for Reed. Instead of picking Captain Rubber or Stretch-O or Super Flubber,

he comes up with "Mr. Fantastic." Where the
hell did he get *that* one? Not that he did any
better, calling himself the Thing. He might as
well have called himself "Lump of Matter" or
"The Doohickey." But then, what the hell did
he know about being a fancy-pants super hero
back then?

A train rumbled up and Ben stepped into the
waiting car. He didn't know which train it was
or where it was headed. He wasn't riding the
train to go anywhere. He was just riding the train
to get away. Not that it'd do him any good—he
was still the Thing no matter where he went. It
wasn't like he could leave his worries back at
the office. Still, it wasn't fair to expose his
friends to his foul temper after all they'd done
to help him.

He eased himself down, his girth taking up
three of the train's seats. He quickly glanced
around the car—most of the other riders were
busy trying not to make eye contact, so he re-
laxed. He remembered how, when he'd been a
boy on the Lower East Side, he and his buddies
used to ride the subway out to Coney Island on
the weekends, to spend what little money they
had at Steeplechase Park.

Yeah, those were the days. He could almost

taste the saltwater taffy and smell the cotton candy. Suddenly, he knew where he wanted to go. He glanced back up at the train's destination, posted next to the doors. He was on the Brooklyn-bound F train: last stop Coney Island. *Perfect.*

* * *

As he emerged from the subway station, Ben regretted his decision to come out to Coney Island almost instantly. Coney Island was no longer the place of his youth. For one thing, Steeplechase Park no longer existed. It had been torn down long ago, and the few remaining amusement pavilions were shabby affairs, looking even sadder without their neon in the hard light of day.

After the dismay washed over him, he noticed that not all of the touchstones of his boyhood had been erased. The old wooden roller coaster, the Cyclone, was still in operation, looking just like the whitewashed death trap he remembered. And the Nathan's Famous stand was still on the corner of Surf and Stillwell avenues, as was the Wonder Wheel, although the defunct Parachute Ride's armature loomed against the afternoon sky like the skeleton of a giant crown roast.

He walked in the direction of the boardwalk, past a collection of shooting galleries, corn dog stands, and a handful of noisy kiddie rides. The calliope music of his past had been replaced by the over-amplified thud of hip-hop, although the Fun House still had the same old maniacal canned laughter coming out of the grinning clown head.

Although it was still daylight, far from the area's "magic time" of dusk, there were a surprising number of people out riding the roller coaster, wolfing down cotton candy, and trying their hands at the rigged games of chance.

One of the barkers, a portable microphone looped around his neck as if he were an air traffic controller, pointed in his direction. "Hey, mistah! Mistah with the hat! Hey, big fella! You look like a sport! Try and knock over the milk bottles! Dollar a ball! Six for five bucks! Knock over th' bottles an' take home a stuffed animal for the kiddies!"

Ben paused and stared at the pyramid of old-fashioned milk bottles. They appeared to be made out of wood and were painted white. He was all too familiar with this particular scam. The top "milk bottle" was legit, but the bottom two were so heavily weighted with lead shot that it would take a howitzer to knock them over. As a boy, he and his older brother, Dan, had blown enough money to buy all the rinky-dink stuffed toys on display behind the counter three times over.

The barker grinned as Ben stepped forward. "Try your luck! Test your skill and strength! Knock over the milk bottles and you get your pick of the prizes!" He gestured grandly to the vast array of plush animals adorning the wall behind him. "Dollar a ball. Six fer five. How many ya want, mistah?"

"Gimme one." Ben tossed a dollar onto the counter before the barker had a chance to see his hands.

"Just one? You sure about that, big feller?"

"Yeah. I'm sure."

Instead of taking the ball the barker offered him, Ben picked up one from the pitching gutter. The barker watched him, not trying to hide the smirk on his face. As far as he was concerned, Ben knew, this big fat guy was just another fish to be cleaned.

Ben didn't bother with an elaborate windup. As it was, the ball flew from his hand with such force that it sent the weighted milk bottles flying like bowling pins. The barker yelped and ducked when one of them narrowly missed his head. Directly behind where the pyramid had stood was a baseball-sized hole punched in the wall.

Ben turned to study the toys hanging behind the barker, whose face had taken on the color of old oatmeal and was shaking like a leaf. "I get my pick of what you got, right?"

The barker nodded silently, his throat mike forgotten.

"I'll take that one," Ben said, pointing at a pink plush sheepdog the size of a three-year-old child.

"S-sure, mistah. T-take whatever you want—j-just don't ever come back t'my booth, okay?" the barker pleaded, handing over the toy .dog.

"Whatever you say, buddy," Ben agreed. As he turned around, he was surprised to see he had drawn a crowd of ten people, all of them staring at him with a mixture of curiosity and speculation.

Way to go, Grimm! You come out here to get some time to yourself, and what do you do— immediately call attention to yourself by pulling a bonehead play in public!

"Here y'go, kid—knock yerself out," he muttered, shoving the stuffed animal at a freckle-faced little girl in a Mickey Mouse T-shirt, shorts, and flip-flops. The child staggered under the weight of her gift, which was half as big as she was. She stared him right in the face for a split second, but didn't break into tears or seem scared. Ben didn't want to question his luck on that count, and turned back toward the boardwalk.

"Tell the nice man thank you, Molly," the little girl's mother prodded.

"Thank you, Mister Super Hero!" Molly called out after him.

For the first time all day, Ben Grimm smiled.

* * *

Ben stood on the boardwalk and stared out at the Atlantic Ocean. It was late in the season, and the beach was less crowded than he remembered it from his childhood. Then again, things had changed since then. Traveling to other vacation spots was a whole lot easier now than it had been back then. More people had cars than when he was coming up. More money and more spare time, as a rule, too. Back in the old days, everyone came out to Coney Island for the summer—the rich, the poor, the in-between. Now it seemed that the beach was mostly the province of the poor and the elderly, and the predators that preyed on unwary revelers.

Back when he was a kid, he and Dan used to scour the sand under the boardwalk, searching for loose change that might have slipped between the cracks. Something told him that far less innocent activities now took place under his feet. Personally, he'd rather grapple with the likes of Doc Doom or Annihilus than the muggers that infested the city.

He'd grown up hard but honest, coming of age on the Lower East Side. His folks had been poor when it came to their pocketbooks, but rich in dignity. His Grandpa Grimm had been famous as a backroom bare-knuckle boxer. His pop had been a stevedore, working the nearby docks, while his mama took in washing to make ends meet. His old man had always been rough on both him and Dan, but it wasn't because he didn't love them. It was just that he'd come home so tired, and start drinking right off the bat to try and relax. After Dan was killed in a gang rumble, pop's drinking got harder—until the day he fell asleep on the couch with a lit cigar and started the fire that killed both him and his wife, leaving Ben orphaned at the age of fifteen.

After his parents were buried, Ben was sent to live with his Uncle Jake, his father's older brother. Jake was the first Grimm to really make something of himself. He'd left behind the poverty of Yancy Street to become a successful doctor with a practice on the Upper West Side. He and his first wife, Alyse, had volunteered to take Ben in. Back then he was still a wiseacre punk running with the Yancy Street Gang. Jake was the one who'd insisted that Ben go back to school, the one who talked him into quitting the street gang, the one who saw greatness in him. Jake wanted him to have a future outside the grimy environs of Yancy Street, and encouraged his interest in playing high-school football— something he proved to have a natural talent for.

Jake had been so proud when he won that football scholarship! He could still remember how his uncle had stood up and applauded when he went up to take his diploma. Jake had faith in him, believed in him, even when he didn't deserve it. He would always love Jake for that.

Going off to the university had been scary, though. It had taken more courage to get on the bus at Port Authority than it had to climb into Reed's experimental rocket years later. He'd always been something of an outsider, no matter what the situation. Back on Yancy Street he was the intelligent, thoughtful boy surrounded by no-neck thugs and shiftless ne'er-do-wells. But now at the university he was the coarse, rough-and-tumble inner city kid surrounded by students who were all better educated, better bred, and better off than himself. His first semester was pure hell. He'd felt so alienated and homesick, he'd come dangerously close to hopping the first bus back to New York more than once. Then, during his second semester, he was assigned a new roomie—a boy genius who used fifteen dollar words the way his Uncle Sidney scratched himself.

It's funny how friendships work. At first glance one wouldn't have thought these two mismatched undergrads would be able to exchange simple hellos, much less live together. But Reed Richards quickly became Ben's best and closest friend. After graduation, Ben joined the Air Force and went on to become one of the best test pilots in the business. His name was mentioned in the same breath as Chuck Yeager, Gus Grissom, and Alan Shepard. It broke his heart when he was passed over for NASA's astronaut program. Apparently the Right Stuff didn't include coming from an urban working-poor background and having a smart mouth.

But then, just when he thought his chance of ever getting to be an astro-jockey were nixed for good, his old buddy Reed had popped back up, armed with the plans for his own privately funded rocket ship. Turned out that Reed had been forced to take government funding in order to create his dream rocket—only to find the project being maneuvered out from under him. The Pentagon paper pushers were claiming that the rocket was unsafe and were shutting the mission down. Reed thought that if he managed to launch the rocket on his own and proved its safety, the boys with the brass buttons would be forced to continue the funding.

Looking back on it, all Ben could think was that they must have been crazy as bedbugs. What had possessed him to agree to try to orbit the world in an untested rocket? Reed serving as co-pilot wasn't all that hare-brained—after all, it was his baby. If anything went wrong, he'd be the man to fix it. But taking along his fiancée and her teenaged kid brother? *That* was hare-brained.

Although they soon lost control of their craft and ended up crash-landing, they survived to tell the tale. They could have very well ended up like poor ol' Gus or the *Challenger* crew. Instead, they emerged with strange, freakish powers born from their exposure to the cosmic rays that had bombarded their unshielded rocket. Suddenly Suzie could make herself disappear and project powerful, invisible force fields just by concentrating. Johnny's body spontaneously combusted without the flames devouring his flesh. Reed could bend and stretch every inch of his anatomy into all kinds of impossible shapes. And Ben—well, he got real ugly and real strong.

He'd given up reading his own fan mail long ago. He still got bags of it every week, most of it addressed to the Thing rather than to Benjamin Grimm, even though none of them had kept their names a secret, like so many other super heroes. He'd tried answering it himself, back when the Fantastic Four were starting out, but it quickly became too much for him. Besides, some of the letters upset him. Not that the person writing him was deliberately trying to provoke him. He paid a nice little old lady out in Yonkers to handle the replies for him. She had standardized form letters for different situations, a stack of "personalized" eight-by-ten-inch photos and a stamp bearing his signature, which she used to sign the responses. Every now and then she'd forward a letter on to him, if she thought it warranted special attention. Usually they were from terminally ill children or the severely handicapped.

The letters that irked him most were the ones that started off, "I wish I could be as strong as you," as if being as strong as a herd of elephants was a good thing. That it was really wonderful not to have to take guff from anyone. They obviously thought his strength was something he could turn on or off, like water from a tap. It never occurred to these people that he spent his days living in dread of accidentally crushing someone's fingers simply by shaking hands. They didn't understand that every piece of furniture in his apartment was specially designed and manufactured, at great personal expense, to withstand his weight and strength. They didn't understand the terror he felt every time he was asked to hold a baby for a photo op. He was the Thing—one of the strongest men on the face of the Earth, and that was cool.

He'd mastered his superhuman strength fairly quickly—more out of necessity than anything else. When the Fantastic Four were new, the government had been exceptionally leery of them. If he hadn't gotten his powers under control, they could have very well found themselves listed as threats to national security. They'd had to save the world's bacon more than once, before they were embraced as heroes.

Ben continued strolling down the boardwalk. Going back to the scene of happier days wasn't improving his mood. If anything, it was making him even more gloomy. His attention was drawn by the sound of a man's voice amplified by a handheld microphone.

"Hur-ree! Hur-ree! Hur-ree! Step right up, ladies and gents! Come one, come all to Professor Mombossa's Congress of Human Miracles!"

An older, somewhat fleshy man with oily hair and thick glasses, wearing a straw boater and carrying a bamboo cane, stood on a wooden platform outside a semipermanent structure fronting the boardwalk. Behind him flapped several crudely painted banners depicting a sword swallower, a fat lady, a midget wearing a turban, a tattooed man, and a bearded man with the lower body of a fish. As he spoke about the various performers, he whacked each banner with the cane.

"See! The A-mazing Human Ostrich! He swallows most anything, including swords, lit neon tubes, lightbulbs, nails—even live mice!

See! Lovely Lotta, the two-ton Venus! See! Swami Shorty—the world's smallest mentalist! See! Picture Pete, the pain-proof illustrated man! See! The Wondrous Merman! King of the Seven Seas! All for the price of one percent of a hundred dollars! One hundred pennies! One Father-of-Our-Country! Hur-ree! Hur-ree! Hur-ree! Step right up! The next show starts in just five minutes!''

Ben Grimm stared at the banners. So these guys thought they were freaks, huh? Maybe when compared to Joe Blow from Kokomo—but next to him, they were the Beautiful People. Hell, maybe he ought to buy a ticket and go inside. Maybe when they got a look at him, they'd realize how lucky they were. Maybe he'd even cheer them up. Or maybe he'd just wallow around in self-pity like a prize hog in slop.

The barker—no doubt Professor Mombossa himself—ducked off the bully platform and darted inside the entrance. There were already several people lining up at the ticket booth, dollar bills in hand, as Ben moved to join them. He bought a ticket from a thin, bald young man whose entire head was swarming with tattoos, including the lids of his eyes, and moved into the cool shade of the freak show.

The interior was a large open space with a set of metal bleachers facing a slightly elevated stage. A large canvas wall hid the backstage from view. The place smelled of sweat, half-eaten corn dogs, spilled beer, and cotton candy. The audience filed into the bleachers, but Ben did not follow suit, for fear of collapsing the structure. He stood to one side with his arms crossed over his chest and faced the platform. No one seemed to notice or care.

Professor Mombossa reappeared from behind the canvas flap, and launched into his patented carny spiel concerning the authenticity of the wonders they were about to witness. First they brought out the sword swallower, an underfed young man with dirty blond hair he wore in a ponytail that hung halfway down his back. The audience clapped grudgingly as he swallowed first a sword, then a lit fluorescent light, which caused his trachea to glow.

"There's a trick to how they do that," a large, thickset man wearing a baseball cap announced loudly from the bleachers. He was apparently talking to his wife, a small, birdlike woman with a bad home perm. "He ain't really swallowin' that thing, y'know."

The next act was the midget mentalist. He

was dressed in a tiny formal tuxedo with a turban on his head. Although he wasn't half-bad, as carny mind readers go, he wasn't exactly Professor X, either.

"He ain't no real mind reader. He's using tricks and hand signals. That's how he's doin' it. I seen how they do it on *Geraldo* once," the thick-necked baseball cap was quick to point out.

After Swami Shorty came the fat lady. She was seated on a large, padded, thronelike chair mounted on wheels, and the sword swallower and Professor Mombossa had to wheel her out from behind the canvas onto the stage. She was dressed in a flashy spangled outfit with a fringed skirt and white go-go boots. Her act consisted of singing "These Boots Were Made for Walking" and a passable Kate Smith impersonation.

The tattooed man was up next, and he proved to be the ticket-taker Ben noticed earlier, only this time stripped down to a pair of Speedos. But that was only part of his act. He also drove a nail through his tongue and into a block of wood.

"Look—it's pierced already! He ain't *really* driving a nail through it!" Baseball Cap announced to all and sundry.

Ben was beginning to feel both bored and foolish for having paid to come in by the time Professor Mombossa reappeared. He rapped the platform with his cane to get everyone's undivided attention.

"Ladies and gentlemen! I am about to present to you the latest—and greatest—addition to my Congress of Human Miracles! What you are about to see is not really human! The creature I am speaking of is a beast straight from the myths of ancient Greece! It is none other than a real, live merman! Half man, half fish! Captured off the shores of Crete by surprised fishermen, and brought to this country at great expense and personal danger to yours truly, Professor Mombossa, for your edification and delight! Ladies and gentlemen, it is my proud pleasure to introduce to you—King Neptune, Lord of the Seven Seas!"

The tattooed man and the sword swallower wheeled out a huge glass tank full of water, in which floated a creature with the upper body of a human and the tail of a fish. The mer-man had long dark hair and a long flowing beard, like the pictures of Neptune in history books, and clutched the traditional trident.

"He ain't a *real* fish-man! It's just some guy

in a suit breathing through a tube!'' Baseball Cap piped up from the audience.

Ben sighed in disgust. He really ought to call it a day and head back home. This was proving to be a real waste of time. Still, there was something about the fake merman's face that held his interest. But what? He stared at the man in the tank, whose features were partially obscured by a fake beard. Then King Neptune turned his gaze away from the audience and in his direction. There was anger and confusion in those eyes—and when they fell on Ben's lumpy figure, a dim glimmer of recognition.

''Oh my God.'' Ben was so shocked, it came out a whisper. ''*Namor.*''

He was moving toward the tank before he realized what he was doing. Professor Mombossa looked startled at the sight of the large, strange man lumbering toward his prize exhibit. ''Sir, I'm afraid I'll have to ask you to retake your seat.''

''Stuff it, Booze-O, or whatever it is you call yourself,'' Ben growled, pushing the carny out of the way. ''I don't know what you're trying to pull, but this guy's a friend of mine!''

''Don't worry, honey!'' Baseball Cap told his wife. ''The big guy's all part of the act!''

"Pete! Ostrich! We got trouble!" Mombossa yelled, and the sword swallower and tattooed man ran out from behind the curtain, baseball bats in hand. The sword-swallower took a swing at Ben, knocking off his hat. There was a collective gasp from the audience as they saw his face.

"Lookit, honey! It's that there super hero—what'sis name! The Hulk!"

"That's it, buddy!" Ben roared, pointing his finger in the direction of Baseball Cap. "It ain't enough I gotta listen to you yammer—now you gotta go and insult me!"

Seeing that Ben's back was turned, the sword swallower took another swing at him with the bat, splintering it against the back of his head. The Thing turned in his direction.

"You tryin' to get my attention, buddy?"

The sword swallower threw down the shattered remains of the bat and fled through the curtain. The tattooed man dropped his weapon and followed suit. When Ben turned around, Professor Mombossa was nowhere to be seen, although most of the audience was still sitting in the bleachers, uncertain whether or not it was all part of the show.

"Ladies and gents, unless you want to buy

new clothes, I'd recommend leaving—'cause it's about to get *real* wet in here!'' He made a fist and pulled back his arm. ''Okay, I don't want any of you sayin' I didn't warn ya! So watch out, folks! *It's clobberin' time!*''

The tank's three-inch-thick glass shattered as if made of spun sugar, unleashing a thousand square feet of water. The deluge sluiced off the platform toward the bleachers, knocking Ben off his feet. The remaining audience members screamed and ran for cover as the wall of water crashed into the seats like a small-scale tidal wave.

''Awww—cripes! My good coat!'' Ben groaned as he picked himself up. He was soaked from head to toe, with empty popcorn bags and discarded cigarette butts glued to his back and sleeves. Then he remembered the Sub-Mariner and swiveled around, looking for the Atlantean. ''Namor? Where are you, fish cake?''

He spied Namor's limp body at the foot of the platform, still tricked out in that ridiculous sea-king costume, lying facedown in a pool of filthy water. He didn't like the way Namor was just laying there like—well, like a dead fish. He hurried over to where the Sub-Mariner lay sprawled and rolled him over.

"Namor—what's going on here? What were you doin' in that lousy tank? Why'd that guy have you dressed up like the Little Mermaid?"

Namor was looking right at him, but Ben could tell he was seeing something else entirely. Even though his sense of touch was far from subtle, he could tell that the Atlantean was feverish.

"Vashti—" he croaked. "Byrrah—Kreeg . . . Beware—"

"And 'Klaatu barada nikto' to you too, pointy-ears. Seems like I picked the right day to wallow in self-pity, huh? C'mere, lemme help you outta this stupid getup." The rubber fishtail came away in his hands like crepe paper, as did the dimestore wig and fake beard.

Namor gasped and began to spasm, his body flopping about like a landed fish. Ben realized the Sub-Mariner had somehow lost his ability to breathe air. He quickly lifted the stranded merman in his arms and hurried in the direction of the exit and the ocean front beyond its threshold.

A crowd of curious onlookers clustered around the front of the freak show, attracted by the pandemonium coming from inside. Upon the appearance of the Thing on the boardwalk, the curiosity seekers quickly dispersed in all directions, not wanting to get in the man's way.

No one tried to block Ben's path as he made his way down the steps to the beach, either, although several startled sunbathers looked up at the sight of a huge, thickset man dressed in a sopping wet camel-hair coat, carrying what looked to be a dead man in his arms, wading out into the surf.

"I don't know if I'm doin' the right thing here," Ben said aloud to the unconscious Sub-Mariner as he lowered him into the water. "Reed's the one who knows about these things, not me. But I watched this documentary on PBS last week—about marine biologists savin' some whales that beached themselves."

Keeping one hand on the ailing Sub-Mariner so the tide did not wash him out to sea, Ben fumbled with his wristwatch, activating the pre-programmed alert message. The watch resembled the kind of timepiece favored by sport divers, but it was one of Reed's little inventions. A genuine two-way wrist TV, just like Dick Tracy's. Except this one also had a microcomputer with enough memory to do Willie Nelson's taxes built in. The liquid crystal display flickered for a moment, to be replaced by a tiny Mr. Fantastic face.

"Ben? Are you all right? Where are you? We received your SOS but I haven't locked in on your position yet."

"I'm at Coney Island, Reed. But I ain't the one in trouble. It's our ol' buddy, the Sub-Mariner!"

Reed frowned. "Namor? At Coney Island? What in heaven's name is he doing *there*?"

"Beats me, but I'm bettin' he didn't stop by for the corn dogs! Somethin' fishy's goin' on— no pun intended. He's in a bad way. His lungs ain't workin'. Reed—I think he's dyin'!"

Mr. Fantastic was silent for a second. Ben knew what was running through his old friend's head. He and Namor had long been at odds with one another. As if their basic natures being diametrically opposed wasn't enough—Reed being the cool, analytical type, the master of his intellect; Namor, the brash, arrogant warrior-king, ruled by his emotions—Namor's long-standing fascination with Sue didn't help matters.

"Stay with him, Ben. I'll be there as soon as possible. We'll use the Fantasti-Car to evac him back to the Plaza."

The LCD went back to telling the time and Ben heaved a sigh. Something told him he was on the verge of being swept into another life-or-death adventure. Oh, well. At least it'd keep him from being a self-pitying fool for a few days.

* * *

The Fantasti-Car—a specially designed jet craft using vertical take-off technology designed by Reed—arrived from Manhattan ten minutes later. And not a second too soon, as far as Ben was concerned.

A huge crowd of rubberneckers had gathered on the beach and boardwalk, gawking at the sight of the world-famous Thing standing up to his waist in the Atlantic Ocean in his civvies, apparently drowning a man by holding his head under water.

A shadow passed over the assembled onlookers. Then a powerful wind, like that of a dozen helicopters, began blowing the beach umbrellas, blankets, and sand in every direction. The crowd cried out in alarm and ran for the protection of the boardwalk as the Fantasti-Car settled on the now-empty stretch of beach.

The Thing waved at Mr. Fantastic, seated behind the controls of the craft. Mr. Fantastic returned the signal and popped the cockpit canopy. Without moving from the flight deck, he stretched his torso out to where Ben stood in the surf. In one hand he held a full-body containment suit and helmet normally used for those occasions when the Fantastic Four had to travel into space. Composed of the same unstable molecules as their costumes, it allowed the team to use their various powers without fear of exposing themselves to environments hostile to oxygen-breathing carbon-based lifeforms.

"Here, put this on him," Reed explained, handing the suit to Ben. "I altered it so that it will supply Namor with freshly aerated water in place of oxygen."

"Where are Suzie and Johnny?" Ben asked as he stuffed the Sub-Mariner's limp body into the suit. It was like trying to put jammies on a sleeping kid while standing in the surf-pool at Wet 'n' Wild.

"I've got them busy setting up a 'hospital' for our sick friend here." Reed placed his fingers against Namor's throat to take his pulse. The look of his face was a mixture of scientific curiosity and genuine concern. "You weren't joking. I'm not up on my Atlantean biology, but one thing is for certain: he *is* dying."

Ben shook his head in amazement. "I never thought I'd see the day when you backed up my diagnosis." He placed the clear plastic bubble-helmet over Namor's head and locked it in place. Water immediately flooded the helmet, although Namor still showed no signs of consciousness.

"Let's get him in the Fantasti-Car. We don't have any time to waste if we're going to try and keep him alive."

"I got 'im," the Thing grunted, lifting the Sub-Mariner over his shoulder in a fireman's carry. As he slogged his way back toward land, he made a mental note to call his shoemaker and tailor when he got home. He was going to have to kiss this coat and pair of shoes goodbye after today's little adventure in the surf and sand.

The side of the Fantasti-Car opened and a metal loading ramp dropped down. Reed appeared in the hatchway and stretched out one of his arms to help relieve him of his burden.

"That's him, officer! That's him! That's the creature that disrupted my show, attacked my performers, and stole my main attraction!"

Professor Mombossa was trying to hurry across the sandy beach, pointing in the Thing's direction, a befuddled beat cop in tow.

"Oh, great," Ben grumbled. "Reed, you take Namor while I deal with this two-bit Barnum."

Professor Mombossa dodged behind the police officer as Ben turned to face him. "I-I demand that you arrest him, officer!"

The cop glanced over his shoulder at Mombossa and then at the Thing. He cleared his throat. It was obvious he wanted to be anywhere but where he was. "Uh, is what this, um, gentleman saying true, Mister—uh—?"

"Grimm."

"Yeah. I figured that's, uh, who you were. Well, did you attack this man and, uh, damage his place of business?"

"Yeah. You could say that. Except that Bozo here didn't tell you that his boys came after me with baseball bats *first*. Or that the 'main attraction' I'm accused of stealin' was a prisoner bein' held against his will!"

"That's not true!" Mombossa retorted, "I found him! He's mine!"

"He's the freakin' *ruler* of Atlantis! You can't go stickin' heads of state in big glass jars an' charge people a dollar to gawk at 'em! Or do you have Queen Elizabeth in a jar, too? And, buddy, I've known the Sub-Mariner a hell of a lot longer than you have, and I can tell you he didn't agree to wear a stupid Halloween suit for beer money!"

The police officer turned to scowl at Mombossa, who now looked as though he wanted to burrow his way into the sand. "What the hell were you doin' with this Sub-Mariner guy, Professor?"

"You don't have anything on me! He ain't human, so it's not like he's a slave or kidnapped!"

Ben leaned forward and pointed a blunt, rocky finger at Mombossa. "Mister, it's sorry scum like you that makes me have to apologize for bein' human—or havin' been one. You can go ahead and have me arrested, if you want— but just be ready to find yourself up on federal kidnapping and unlawful imprisonment charges! Mebbe even negligent homicide if my friend there dies."

"D-dies? Uh, look, big guy—I didn't do nothin' to him, see? He was like that when I found 'im, a couple of days ago. He's been sick since I first laid eyes on 'im! You can't blame that on me!"

"C'mon, Professor," the cop growled, clamping a beefy hand on Mombossa's upper arm. "We're goin' to the station house for a nice long talk. Sorry about the misunderstanding, Mr. Grimm. I'll see that the report gets written up correctly. C'mon you."

Professor Mombossa sullenly watched the Fantasti-Car as it streaked across the sky in the direction of Manhattan, carrying his one and only chance at fame and fortune in its belly.

"It ain't fair," he mumbled under his breath. "Finders keepers."

CHAPTER 3

TO SAVE A KINGDOM

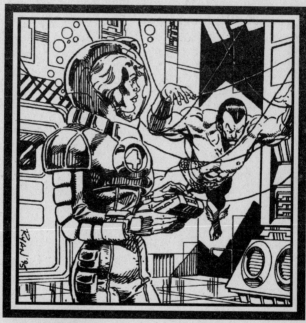

The top of Four Freedom's Plaza opened like a blooming nightflower as the Fantasti-Car approached, exposing the combination hangar and launchpad that occupied the skyscraper's upper level. The moment the aircraft touched down, the Human Torch ran up to it, yelling over the din of the engines as they powered down.

"Sue's in the lab, overseeing the last-minute touches on the isolation chamber! We set it up per your instructions!"

"Good," Reed said with a curt nod. "We don't have any time to spare! We've got to get Namor hooked up to life support ASAP!"

Ben lumbered out of the belly of the Fantasti-Car, cradling Namor's limp body in his massive arms. Johnny stared at the Sub-Mariner's waxen face, shaking his head in amazement.

* * *

Sue was waiting for them in the lab, dressed in a suit similar to the one Namor was wearing, the helmet tucked under one arm. She gasped at the sight of the regal Sub-Mariner clutched in the Thing's arms like a rag doll.

"Dear Lord! Reed, is he—?"

"Dead? No. Not yet, anyway."

"It's so strange to see him like this. Normally he's so vigorous, so in control of himself . . ."

"Yeah," Ben grunted. "I know what you mean. I've never considered ol' fish face a close personal friend, but I never thought of him as an enemy—not like Doom or Annihilus or even poor ol' Mole Man! Seein' him like this kinda, I dunno, scares me a little. Hell, who am I kiddin'? It scares me a *lot*!"

"Did you finish converting the isolation chamber?" Reed asked his wife.

Sue nodded. "I just finished sterilizing and flooding the chamber. The life-support leads are in place and activated. Johnny double-checked the welding. The room's watertight.''

The isolation chamber was normally reserved as a holding cell for the various human villains or alien miscreants the Fantastic Four ran across. The walls were six feet thick and reinforced with titanium alloy, which rendered them virtually impregnable. Allowing for the various forms of life wandering the galaxy, the chamber could be flooded with ammonia, carbon dioxide, chlorine—or water.

Sue punched the code on the airlock that opened onto the isolation chamber and placed the helmet over her head. She then pressed a button on the suit's chest-plate, activating a hidden speaker. "I'll take over from here, boys.''

"Y'sure about that, Suzie?" Ben asked, as he handed the unconscious Sub-Mariner over to the petite blonde woman. "He ain't exactly whisper-thin, y'know.''

"I realize that, Ben. But I can generate a force field to help support Namor's weight.''

With that, she linked her arms under the Sub-Mariner's, and moved him into the airlock as easily as she would a child. She waved to her brother, who shut the door behind her and keyed in the code for the inner door to open, flooding the airlock.

Ben and the others moved to the one-way observation port and watched the Invisible Woman as she carefully peeled away the Sub-Mariner's containment suit and maneuvered him into the life-support web floating in the middle of the chamber. The Thing shook his head in wonder.

"Where do I come off playin' the big, bad macho dude, huh? I mean—part of it's how I was raised, y'know? Y'open doors for dames. Y'walk on the outside when yer goin' down the street. That kinda stuff. I keep thinkin' that because she's this little slip of a girl, she can't do the donkey work. But look at her! Suzie could hammer my rocky butt into the pavement any day of th' week without breakin' a sweat!"

Reed nodded absently as he sat down in front of the central diagnostic computer that was tied into the life-support web in the isolation chamber. He began typing in commands on the computer's keyboard, his fingers stretching to lengths professional typists only dream of. "I've accessed what little information there is concerning Atlantean physiology, plus that of all sea mammals and fish. Taking Namor's human father into account, checking for possible genetic disorders that might explain his condition . . .''

The movie-screen-sized video monitor mounted on the wall flickered and a magnetic resonance image of the Sub-Mariner sprang into view. Reed frowned at the pulsating multicolored swirls that represented Namor's beating heart, kidney functions, and brain activity.

He wished he had a true physician present. Such medical knowledge would be of great help in this situation. Lacking such expertise, he was forced to operate on the assumption that Atlantean and human biology were not *that* different. After all, Namor's parents had managed to produce a viable—one would say exceptional—offspring. And, if what Namor had once hinted about the origins of his people was correct, the Atlanteans were once human before undergoing some strange form of mutagenic process, made possible by an ancient form of technology long since lost, in order to breathe underwater and withstand the extreme pressure and cold of the ocean floor.

Still, he did have the resources of one of the finest research laboratories on the face of the earth at his fingertips, and once presented with a problem—whether it was something as simple as a Rubik's Cube or the question of rebuffing an attack from Galactus—Reed Richards dedicated himself to it completely and didn't let up until it was solved.

* * *

Sue Richards looked through her helmet at the face of the only man besides her husband who'd ever pledged his undying love to her.

Namor was exceptionally handsome, if in an exotic fashion, with his arched eyebrows, pointed ears, and high cheekbones. She had been little more than a girl at the time they first met. *God, those days seemed so long ago!* The Fantastic Four were in their embryonic stages, and she was still calling herself the Invisible Girl. She was also unmarried when Namor first flew into her life on those strange winged feet of his.

She'd considered him attractive from the very first, but his physical appearance was a minor part of her fascination with Namor. She was drawn to his self-confidence and sense of justice, qualities that had also attracted her to Reed. But their similarities ended there. The fierce, savage passion Namor possessed was a stark contrast to Reed's intellectual reserve. Namor had begged her to leave the surface world and become his queen in Atlantis. And she had been tempted—far more than she would ever be able to confess to Reed.

In the end, she had declined Namor in favor of Reed. Namor took the rejection well enough, although he continued to press his case over the years. And in many ways, it had been his feelings for her that eventually tempered his hostility to those he contemptuously referred to as "air-breathers."

Despite their initial mistrust, Reed, Ben, and Johnny developed a grudging respect for the Atlantean noble. For all his quarrelsomeness, Namor was hardly a villain like Dr. Doom. But of all the Fantastic Four, only she held a soft spot for the outspoken merman.

No doubt the boys' egos got in their way of understanding the Sub-Mariner the way she did. Where they saw hauteur and braggadocio, Sue saw a man bound by the ancient protocols of a culture drowned before the dawn of recorded time. If he often treated those about him as inferiors and angered quickly when he did not immediately get his way, it was only because such concepts as "democracy" and "equality" were still novelties to one born to the purple. Despite his initial savagery, Sue had sensed the Sub-

Mariner's true nature from the first time he looked into her eyes. Namor possessed true greatness; his was a hero's soul.

She shook herself free of her reverie, cursing herself for drifting away from the job at hand. There would be plenty of time for memories later. His fever was raging and, except for an occasional feeble movement, he was completely still. Every now and again he would make a noise that sounded like the ultrasonic chatter of porpoises. She removed the medi-kit clipped to her belt and flipped it open. She had to take blood and tissue samples for diagnosis. She knew from previous experience that Namor's skin was deceptively thick—she'd personally witnessed bullets ricochet off him.

She selected the special syringe reserved for those rare occasions when the Thing required medical attention. It had been built to Reed's specifications by Stark Enterprises, using a special titanium alloy. She drove the hypodermic into Namor's elbow and drew out a syringe full of blood. She was surprised to find it was red. She remembered Namor telling her that Atlantean blood was deep blue or purple.

As she prepared to leave, Namor began muttering and moving his head back and forth in an agitated manner. Sue reached out and touched his feverish brow, stroking it with her gloved fingers.

"Hush, now. It's okay. You're amongst friends."

Namor continued to mutter, but his struggling ceased. Sue swam back to the airlock with the sample, but before she entered, she looked back at him one last time.

* * *

Sixteen hours later, after running all the diagnostic tests he possibly could on their house guest, Mr. Fantastic summoned the rest of the Fantastic Four to the laboratory. They found him seated where they had last seen him, in front of the central computer. He had neither shaved, showered, slept, nor eaten during that time. Reed was like that. Needless to say, he did not realize that his call had come at three in the morning.

Ben came stomping into the lab dressed in a red silk bathrobe as big as a tent, his feet encased in fuzzy pink slippers. "What's the hubbub, bub?" he yawned.

"Yeah," Johnny chimed in, trying to stifle his own yawn. He was wearing a terrycloth half-coat and plaid boxers. His blond hair was so tousled his cowlick was standing straight up.

"This better be good, brother-in-law. I was dreaming about Claudia Schiffer when you buzzed."

"Reed? You never came to bed." Sue faded into view at her husband's elbow, clutching her chiffon negligee. "Did you find something?"

"Indeed I did, darling," Reed said again. "I discovered the nature of Namor's illness."

The computer's video screen was filled with what looked like a blood sample as seen under a microscope.

"There is our culprit," Reed said, using the clicker on his mouse to enlarge a portion of the screen.

The other members of the team stared blankly at what looked like a gaggle of spiny soap bubbles beating up on a bunch of smooth soap bubbles.

"That's real nice, Stretch—but what the Sam Hill are we lookin' at?" Ben asked.

"A virus. Interesting, no?" Reed asked, watching the pulsating blobs with the detached appreciation of an art historian.

Johnny scratched his head and shot Ben a confused look. "Uh, could you give us a little more information? I'm afraid the rest of us aren't up on our microbiology."

"Hmm? Oh, of course. I'm sorry. Viruses are classified on the basis of their nucleic acid content, their size, the shape of their protein coat, and the presence of a surrounding lipoprotein membrane. What you're looking at are enveloped virions about one hundred nanometers in diameter with helical nucleocapsid containing eight segments of negative-strand RNA and endogenous RNA polymerase. The lipoprotein envelope contains two glycoproteins, designated hemaglutinin and neuraminidase, which puts it in the family Orthomyxoviridiae—"

"C'mon, Stretch, quit bustin' my chops! Give it to us in English, okay?"

"Very well. He has the flu."

Johnny's jaw dropped. "The *flu*?!? C'mon, brother-in-law—! Look at him! How could he just have the flu?"

"This is hardly a case of 'just' having the flu, Johnny. What Namor is suffering from is, to be more accurate, viral pneumonia accompanied by influenza. Bear in mind that the influenza has claimed far more lives than all the wars of this century. From 1918 to 1919, over twenty-five million people died from the disease."

"Whoa!" Johnny returned his gaze to the screen, stunned by the sheer numbers.

"After eighteen months, and having achieved such dubious accomplishments as diminishing the Eskimo population by sixty percent and ravaging Spain so horribly that it became known as the 'Spanish Influenza,' despite having originated in the United States, the bug vanished as quickly as it first appeared. It disappeared so thoroughly from the face of the Earth that no modern-day microbiologist has been able to find a specimen for study. Until today."

"Are you saying that Namor is sick with a disease that disappeared over seventy-five years ago?" Johnny marveled, scratching his head. "How can that possibly be?"

"Flu viruses are notorious for their rapid mutations and corresponding migrations into new populations. These changes occur every couple of years, and involve only minor changes in the outer coat of the virus. Most immune systems are able to recognize the variation and combat it fairly effectively. However, every decade or so a major antigenic drift occurs, during which the virus's spiky protein coat changes so dramatically that most human immune systems cannot recognize the virus and fight it off.

"However, what we're looking at is not

such a virulent mutagenic shift. This is an *artificial* virus, one specially manipulated to replicate the original Spanish Influenza as closely as possible.

"Yeesh," Ben muttered. "Why'd anyone wanna make a new flu?"

"It's worse than that, Ben," Reed said. "It seems to have been specifically designed to target Namor's system, and no other's. Apparently, our would-be regicide had access to Namor's tissue. The virus was built to be lethal—but not instantaneously so. It was to look like a natural illness, not a poisoning. However, Namor's amphibious nature bought him the necessary time for us to affect a cure. His lungs are severely inflamed and blocked with fluid—but the membranes that allow him to breathe underwater are still operating. If Namor was human, he would have died within days—perhaps even hours—of his initial exposure. No doubt his enemies did not expect him to live so long."

"Disease as a means of assassination!" Sue marveled aloud. "And from someone who had access to a tissue sample. It would have to be someone in Atlantis, someone close to him."

"A reasonable hypothesis, Sue, but there's one more piece to this puzzle. Here, allow me to enlarge the magnification . . .'' Suddenly the spiny blob grew several thousandfold, revealing a glistening surface marred by a series of narrow dark stripes at the right-hand corner.

"Hey—what're those marks on one end of Mr. Yuck, there?" Ben said, pointing at the screen. "They almost look like—"

"A magnetic pricing code? You're very close, Ben. It's a bio-engineered identification patch. A patent number, if you will."

"Patent!?! You can patent a freakin' germ!?!"

"Indeed you can, old friend. And it's a growing business. I've already checked the registration for this particular piece of dirty work. It's registered to a company called Bio-Industriales. The head office is located in Latveria."

Johnny slapped his forehead and rolled his eyes in disgust. "Can our panel name tonight's arch-villain in four letters or less?"

"Doom," grumbled Ben darkly.

"Bingo!"

"I shoulda known. But why would the Doomster be interested in snuffin' ol' Subby? Granted, they've butted heads more than once, but I kind of thought he spent most of his spare time figgerin' out ways to deep-six us."

"I have no idea why Doom should want Namor dead," Reed sighed, running a hand across the stubble on his chin. "But I can guarantee you that whatever interest our old enemy has in Atlantis cannot be healthy. Von Doom does nothing that does not benefit him in some way."

"Are you sure it *is* Doom, Reed?" Sue asked. "Just because the company's based in Latveria doesn't necessarily mean that Doom is involved."

"I doubt there's anything that goes on in Latveria that Von Doom *isn't* involved in, Sue. Furthermore, the level of sophistication here is far beyond any other patents registered to Bio-Industriales. And, frankly, Doom is one of the only people on the planet capable of creating so sophisticated a virus."

Sue rubbed her chin thoughtfully. "That doesn't answer how Doom got his hands on a tissue sample of Namor's. Unless he's in cahoots with someone in Atlantis with designs on the throne."

"When I got 'im outta the tank," Ben said, "Subby mumbled somethin' 'bout Vashti, Byrrah, and Kreeg. Dunno about Kreeg, but ain't Byrrah his cuz?"

"Yes," Sue said, "and the heir to the throne should anything happen to Namor."

"It's possible there's a coup being planned, though for now we can only speculate as to Von Doom's motives for being involved," Reed said. "Right now our next step is to try to cure Namor and see if he can shed some light on the situation.

"Unlike bacteria, viruses mimic the metabolic functions of their host cells. Antibiotics and other antimicrobial agents are, therefore, ineffective against them because the chemical compounds that inhibit the reproduction of viruses also slow the functions of—or are actually toxic to—the host. However, certain artificial compounds, such as ribavirin, acyclovir, and azidothymidine have proven effective in improving, if not curing, viral diseases without toxic side effects. This will at least provide me with a jumping-off point in an attempt to generate a serum that will halt the killer virus and allow Namor's immune system to recuperate . . ."

"Well, you do that, Reed," Ben yawned. "I'll be takin' a snooze if you need any heavy lifting done. And if you don't mind me buttin' in, High Pockets, you could probably stand a few winks yourself."

Sue leaned over her husband's shoulder, placing her hand atop his own. "Ben's right, darling—you haven't slept in over twenty-four hours. Won't you please come to bed?"

"Hmm?" Reed looked away from the arcane figures scrawling across the computer screen. "Did you say something, dear?"

His eyes were red-rimmed and the creases at their corners were deep enough to appear chiseled into his face, but Sue knew that look all too well. She smiled tightly and pecked him on the cheek.

"Just promise me you won't work yourself into another nervous collapse."

"Hmm?"

"Never mind, sweetheart."

CHAPTER 4

ESCAPE
FROM ATLANTIS

Prince Byrrah stood on the balcony overlooking the Great Plaza, watching the citizens of Atlantis as they placed mourning wreaths at the foot of the statue of their departed lord, Namor I. Most of the populace seemed genuinely bereft, some even going so far as to rend their garments, cut off their hair, and shave their beards as tokens of grief. As he watched his subjects file past the monument to their dead ruler, it was all he could do to supress a smile.

At last! After all those years of frustration, the crown was finally his! After a lifetime of being second best to his insufferable cousin, now it was his turn to take charge. And once the people of Atlantis recognized what a brilliant ruler they had in Byrrah, they would soon forget Namor even existed . . .

"Your Highness?"

"What is it, Tydeus?" Byrrah said, his reverie broken.

The corpulent Viscount of Charybdis was fidgeting with his waist-sash, which Byrrah had come to recognize as a sign that Tydeus was being forced to do something he'd rather not. Although he had proven extremely helpful as a co-conspirator, Byrrah found the Atlantean noble both pompous and tedious. Tydeus had hinted broadly that he expected to be rewarded for his part in Namor's downfall by being made Chief Chamberlain, replacing the aged Vashti. As much as Byrrah disliked the old sea turtle, he could not imagine exchanging him for such a fool as Tydeus.

"There is a delegation that wishes an audience with Your Highness."

"Indeed?" Byrrah sniffed. "Tell them to go away, Tydeus. I'm in mourning for my cousin."

"Somehow I doubt the truth of your words, Byrrah," Vashti snorted as he entered the throne room, accompanied by Seth and Hiordis.

"You dare accuse a prince of the blood of

lying?'' sputtered Tydeus, rising to his master's defense.

"Let us say that I suspect his 'bereavement' has more to do with appearances than actual grief," Vashti commented wryly. "As for myself, I do not believe for one moment that Namor is dead."

"Believe what you like, old man. Namor will remain dead, no matter what," Kreeg said, emerging from his hiding place behind the throne, harpoon in hand. He glowered darkly at Vashti, Seth, and Hiordis, no longer disguising his hatred for them.

"You keep saying that Namor is no more," Seth said, stepping forward. "Yet there is no body. Yours is the only word we have that he is, indeed, dead."

"The entire Seventh Regiment saw him collapse on the reviewing stand," Byrrah exclaimed. "Surely that was no trick! We buried Namor under a cairn near where he died for fear of whatever disease killed him. Surely you could not expect us to bring his corpse back to Atlantis! What if whatever killed him was contagious?" Byrrah was doing his best to look and sound sincere.

"No doubt he contracted his illness from the

air-breathers he was so fond of," Kreeg remarked curtly.

"That's preposterous!" Hiordis retorted. "Namor trafficked with air-breathers for decades and had yet to suffer the slightest illness! Why should he suddenly fall deathly ill now? And if you were so concerned about contagion, why did you return to Atlantis after tending his sickbed? Weren't you two afraid of becoming sick as well?"

"I do not like your tone of voice, half-breed," Kreeg growled. "What is that you are implying? That Prince Byrrah and I had something to do with Namor's demise?"

"I *suggest* nothing, Warlord," Hiordis responded, his words dripping venom. "It is the truth!"

"Save your pretense of loyalty to Namor for the rabble, half-breed!" Kreeg sneered. "You're merely jealous because Prince Byrrah appointed me to replace you as Master-of-Arms of the Royal Guard!"

"You forget one thing, Warlord, that you would do well to remember," Vashti said, his old voice quiet but firm. "Byrrah may very well be next in line to the throne, but his succession is not automatic. The Congress of Lords must first vote to declare him the official ruler. And I plan to see that it does not come to pass—until all questions concerning the death of Namor are resolved to my satisfaction.''

"You wouldn't dare!" Byrrah gasped.

"I am an old man, my prince, and I have little to lose. And let me remind you that Namor was more than my sovereign—he was my friend. And the closest thing I will ever have to a son. If he met his end through foul play, I will see him avenged. Now that we have said what we came here to say, we will take our leave. Good day, Prince Byrrah. I trust I will see you on the floor of the Congress on the morrow.''

Byrrah was too angry to do more than glower at the trio as they left. The moment the throne room doors closed behind them, Tydeus darted forward, his eyes all but starting from his head.

"Your Highness—what are we to do?"

What to do, indeed. Byrrah frowned and stroked his chin and throat. The old crab was right—he needed the approval of the Congress if he was to legally claim the crown. And there was no telling what kind of trouble Vashti could create for him. The old man was well respected and much revered and held a great deal of sway

135

over the courtiers and nobles. If Vashti, Seth, and Hiordis stirred up enough dissent to force him to produce a body . . .

"I say we kill them," Kreeg snarled. "Who cares what the Congress decides anyway? It's only a formality—"

"No!" Byrrah snapped. "I will not have my subjects whispering amongst themselves that I usurped the crown! I am a member of the royal family and the second in line to the throne! I will observe the rituals as tradition demands! And I will not have Vashti and the others assassinated—that would only make things more difficult."

Tydeus began nodding his head. "But if they should be arrested for suspicion of conspiracy? And, without a doubt, they *are* conspiring."

Kreeg could see where Tydeus was going and allowed himself a smile. It was an unpleasant sight. "And, once you are made ruler of Atlantis, your signing the death decree for the execution of known conspirators would not be in any way illegal."

Byrrah did not like the look in Kreeg's eye when he said "execution," but did not call the warlord on it. "No one would believe that

Vashti would ever conspire against Atlantis. Besides, the cantankerous old kraken knows more about the running of the empire than any member of the royal family. No, I want to keep Vashti alive for a while longer. But that doesn't mean he can't be of use to me while locked away in the dungeon.''

Kreeg bowed stiffly, one hand over his heart in the traditional show of fealty. ''Consider it done, my prince.''

* * *

Tydeus was exceptionally pleased with himself as he made his way home. It would only be a matter of time before Byrrah would name him Chief Chamberlain, replacing the ancient Vashti. Although Byrrah was hesitant about naming his cabinet prematurely, Tydeus had no doubt about the size of the prize awaiting him. Perhaps after a few years of service, he would be made a prince of the realm! He could hardly wait until Tethys heard about his good fortune. She would be so proud of him—how could she refuse the marriage proposal of a man about to be made Chief Court Chamberlain of Atlantis?

As he entered his mansion, his young cousin was there to meet him at the door in place of his servants. Despite her emblems of mourning—dark-colored kelp woven into her long red hair and the ritual octopus ink markings on her lovely azure cheeks—Tethys was a vision of the perfect mermaiden he had long dreamt of taking to be his wife.

"Greetings, cousin," she said, helping him to remove the public robes worn by high-born Atlanteans when traversing the sunken city's flooded byways. "How fares Prince Byrrah?"

"As well as can be expected, considering his grief," Tydeus responded. "What has the cook prepared for our dinner tonight?"

"Swordfish steaks with a puree of eel in walrus butter."

"Excellent! I'm famished!" Tydeus grinned, slapping his ample belly.

"You seem in particularly good humor tonight, Tydeus, although all the empire mourns. Why is that?"

"Because, my beloved cousin, you are looking at a man on the verge of attaining his destiny! Within a day or two, I expect to be made Byrrah's new Chief Court Chamberlain."

Tethys frowned. "But isn't Vashti the Chamberlain?"

"Vashti! Phah! He is an old man, unwilling to think new thoughts! Byrrah needs a younger, far more vital Chamberlain to help usher in the new era that is to come. And I'm just the man for the job.''

''Of that I have no doubt, cousin. But why *you*?''

''Let us say that I have an influence on the prince,'' Tydeus chortled.

''But what about Vashti—did he offer to retire in your favor?''

''I'm afraid the old crab has little to say in the matter, my dear. No more than the half-breed Hiordis did when Byrrah replaced him as Master-of-Arms of the Royal Guard.''

''*What*?''

''That's right—Kreeg is Master-of-Arms now! And I suspect he'll be taking Seth's job as well.'' Tydeus leaned forward, his voice dropping to a conspiratorial whisper. ''If you promise not to tell, I will let you in on a little secret. Prince Byrrah has ordered Kreeg to arrest all three of them—Vashti, Hiordis, and Seth—and inter them in the dungeon. He plans to charge them with conspiracy once he is crowned, and have them all put to death!''

Tethys's blue cheeks paled behind their grief-markings. ''D-death?'' she whispered.

''Poor child,'' Tydeus clucked, taking her

hand and stroking it gently. "It must come as a horrible shock to one as innocent as yourself. But it appears that Kreeg uncovered a plot amongst the three to oust Byrrah and usurp the throne in favor of Hiordis! They must be mad to think that the people of Atlantis would accept the half-breed son of a Lemurian as their ruler!"

"Y-yes, cousin," Tethys managed to stammer. "It *is* quite a shock. If you don't mind, I wish to retire early tonight."

"You're not feeling ill, I trust?"

"I'm just—tired—that's all. What with Namor's death—"

"I understand, my dear. Do your best to relax, child. After all, we have Byrrah's coronation to look forward to. You'll want to look your best!"

* * *

Hiordis, late of the Royal Guard, sat alone in his austere soldier's quarters, lost in thought over what had transpired earlier that day. He cursed himself for a fool in allowing Tydeus and Kreeg to anger him so. His mother had always said he'd inherited his father's Lemurian hot-bloodedness, which, coupled with his Atlantean pride, often made for injudicious action. But, damn Byrrah and his co-conspirators for the barracuda they were—he refused to stand idly by and let them get away with murdering his sovereign!

He owed much to Namor, and not just his recently acquired title of Baron. Namor alone, of all Hiordis's contemporaries, knew what it was like to suffer the stigma of mixed blood in Atlantean society. He remembered how, as a boy, he had suffered the schoolyard taunts of bullies who called him a "greenie." Finally, goaded beyond all tolerance, Hiordis had thrown down his study-scrolls and launched himself at his attackers. There was a great deal of scuffling and Hiordis managed to bloody the lead bully's nose, but the tide of the battle quickly turned against him once he lost the element of surprise. Just as he was about to succumb to what would have doubtless been a severe beating at the hands of his tormentors, a pair of pale hands reached into the tangle of angry boys and effortlessly pushed them apart.

"What is the cause of such unseemly behavior?" Namor demanded. "Why are you three fighting with this boy?"

"It's not our fault, Your Highness!" the lead bully whined. "He started it! He hit me in the nose!"

Namor's eyes narrowed and he turned his gaze to Hiordis, who was doing his best to wipe the blood from his own upper lip. "Is this true, boy?"

"Y-yes, sir. But—"

"But what?" Namor queried, crossing his arms over his mighty chest. "There is seldom a good excuse for fighting, but I will listen to an explanation."

"They were calling me names."

Namor's eyebrow lifted. "Is that so? And what were these names they were calling you, boy?"

Hiordis had to clear his throat even to allow the hateful words out of his mouth. His voice was tight and quiet, little more than an angry whisper. "Half-breed."

Namor's eyebrow arched even higher than before and he glanced at the bullies, who were now shuffling their feet and looking as if they wished they were anywhere but there. "Indeed. And what else did they call you?"

"G-greenie, Your Highness. And they said my father was a Lemurian baby-eater."

A glimmer of recognition seemed to cross the prince's face. "Lemurian? Who is your father, boy?"

"Ruahatu the Freedman, Your Highness."

"Then your mother is the Lady Purana, which makes you one of my kinsmen. Greetings, cousin."

"G-greetings, cousin."

Namor turned to the cowering bullies and shook a stern finger at them. "Hear this, you young reprobates! To speak ill to my kinsman is to speak ill to me. A fist raised in anger against him is likewise a threat to the Royal Person! Do I make myself understood?"

"Yes, Your Highness!" they chorused nervously.

"Good. Now leave my presence before I decide I've been too lenient with you!" Namor stood with his hands planted firmly on his hips and watched the trio disappear in an explosion of air bubbles. After he was sure they were gone, he allowed himself a grin and glanced down at young Hiordis.

"Tell me, cousin—what *is* your name?"

"I am called Hiordis, sir."

Namor clapped him on the shoulder and, to the boy's surprise, used the hem of his purple cape to wipe the blood on his upper lip. "You fight well and bravely, young cousin—and in a good cause. Come see my Master-of-Arms when you're older. The Royal Guard can always use brave men.''

Which is exactly what he did when the time came, and now, years later, he was the Master-of-Arms of the Imperial Guard. Or had been, until that morning, when Byrrah replaced him with that bloodthirsty madman, Kreeg. Hiordis knew in his bones that Kreeg and the others were responsible for whatever ill had befallen Namor. And with Vashti and Seth, he meant to prove it before the Congress of Lords.

''Hiordis!''

The hoarse whisper caused him to start from his reverie, his hand automatically going to his sword.

''What? Who calls my name?''

''Over here! At the window! It's me—Tethys!''

Hiordis glanced in the direction of the one window in the room, which was set on a hinge so that it opened inward. He could make out a slender shadow lurking on the other side. Sheathing his sword, he opened the window and Tethys swam in.

''Thank Poseidon I'm not too late!'' she gasped. ''I swam here as fast as I could, but I wasn't sure if I would get here in time!''

"Milady—what is the meaning for your visit? Although I am indeed pleased to see you, why did you insist on making such an—eccentric—entrance?" Hiordis asked, more than a little perplexed.

Tethys looked around anxiously. "Hiordis, I came to warn you! You have to leave Atlantis immediately!"

"Leave Atlantis? Lady Tethys, have you taken leave of your senses?"

"You don't understand—the city is no longer safe for you! My cousin told me that Prince Byrrah has ordered Warlord Kreeg to arrest you, Vashti, and Seth on the grounds of conspiracy. They plan to prove that you three were plotting to overthrow Byrrah and place you on the throne instead."

"No one would believe such lies!"

"Hiordis—don't you understand? It doesn't matter *what* the people believe! Byrrah and the others will do as they like—especially Kreeg! He's under orders to arrest you! His men are probably already on their way here!"

"But your cousin is in league with Byrrah and Kreeg. Why should you risk arrest by coming here to warn me?"

"Because I know everything Tydeus said

about you is a lie! You are a good man, Hiordis, and a loyal Atlantean. I knew that from the moment I first saw you.''

Hiordis's smile was almost shy. ''Really?'' He suddenly found himself painfully close to the comely young mermaiden. He'd never noticed how much her eyes reminded him of moonlight filtered through the surf . . .

''Yes, really,'' she whispered, her gaze moving over his face like a caress.

The sudden pounding on the door made them jump in alarm, their hands inadvertently closing on one another's.

''Hiordis, son of Ruahatu the Lemurian! Open the door! You are under arrest on the charge of conspiracy!''

Hiordis pushed Tethys in the direction of the open window as he drew his sword with his free hand. ''Flee while you still can, milady! I'll see to it you're not followed!''

''No! I'm not leaving without you, Hiordis!'' Tethys cried, grabbing one of the ceremonial harpoons mounted on the wall.

Before Hiordis could protest, the door exploded inward and three of Kreeg's warriors surged into the room, their weapons drawn.

One of the warriors pointed at Tethys.

"Looks like we interrupted the half-breed's fun, lads! Don't worry lass, you'll have a better time with a *real* man!"

"I doubt that," Tethys retorted, and rammed the harpoon through the surprised warrior's chest.

Taken aback by their companion's speedy demise, the remaining warriors were easily dispatched by Hiordis, who moved with the speed and precision of an orca.

"We must hurry—no doubt Kreeg's men are paying Seth an equally unwelcome visit about now," Hiordis said, as he wiped clean his sword. "And by the way, where did you learn to use a harpoon like that?"

"My family might be of noble blood, but we're far from wealthy," Tethys grinned, hoisting her harpoon. "If we wanted to eat, we had to do the hunting ourselves! I used to help my father on the orca and walrus hunts! I'll tell you more about my frontier childhood later—first we must go and try to help Seth!"

They quietly slipped out the window, trying their best to keep to the shadows as they swam in the direction of Seth's villa. As they drew closer they saw what looked to be Seth, his wrists manacled, being led through the streets by a couple of Kreeg's men. Judging by the bruises and swelling on his face, it was obvious that the head general of Atlantis had not surrendered without a fight.

As swiftly and as surely as leopard seals, Tethys and Hiordis struck. Tethys harpooned one of the warriors from behind, while Hiordis tackled the one who remained, slicing open his throat from gill to gill. While both regretted such brutal action, they could not delude themselves. This was war, pure and simple. Hiordis liberated the keys to Seth's manacles from one of the bodies and tossed them to him.

"Hiordis! Praise be to Neptune! I was afraid they'd captured you just as they did Vashti! But who is this with you?"

"The Lady Tethys. Although she is cousin to Tydeus, she is a friend to Atlantis and Namor—and to us! But what was it you said about Vashti? That he's already captured?"

"Aye. The scum that came to arrest me were bragging about it. Since Vashti makes his home in the royal palace, I doubt it was difficult for Kreeg's thugs to arrest him."

Hiordis frowned and shook his head. "There's nothing we can do to help Vashti—at least not right now. The old man is clever enough to keep himself alive for a while. Byr-rah needs him to secure his claim on the throne. But Tethys is right: Atlantis is too dangerous for us.''

Seth nodded. ''We can join the Seventh Regiment. They're as loyal as they come. The other regiments will flock to our banner within a matter of days. But what of your lovely young friend, Hiordis?''

Tethys's soft lips suddenly became firm. ''You're not leaving me behind! I'm going with you two!''

''But, milady!'' Hiordis protested. ''You'll doubtless be branded a traitor! If we're caught, you'll face the same fate as Seth and myself—death by baiting!''

''I'd rather face that than find myself wedded to Tydeus.''

* * *

''*Byrrah! Wake up, you fool! We've been betrayed!*'' Kreeg thundered at the top of his voice as he kicked open the doors to the royal bedchamber.

''What? Kreeg?'' Byrrah groaned, wiping the sleep from his eyes. ''By the Blood of the Twelve—have you gone *mad*? What do you think you're doing waking me up at such an hour?''

''I *said* we've been betrayed!'' Kreeg cried, and for a second Byrrah was afraid the warlord was actually going to drag him out of bed by his throat. He had never seen Kreeg as angry as he was now, and it was indeed a fearsome sight.

''B-betrayed? By whom? What has happened?''

''Seth and Hiordis have escaped, that's what happened!'' Kreeg spat. ''As you would *know* if you hadn't gone to bed!''

''Seth and Hiordis—escaped? But how?''

''In Hiordis's case, he was warned in advance, and then he and his co-conspirator were able to effect Seth's release—killing several of my best men along the way!''

Byrrah frowned. Some of this wasn't making sense, but he wasn't exactly sure which part. ''His co-conspirator? You mean he and Vashti attacked your men?''

''Hardly! Vashti is sitting in the dungeon, where he belongs. No, Hiordis received his help from a young maiden. One of the blood, if what one witness claims is true.''

''Who is this woman?''

Just then there was a loud, angry noise—like

that of penguins arguing over herring—and Tydeus's corpulent bulk was forcefully propelled through the door by a couple of Kreeg's warriors.

"Unhand me, you barbarous cretins!" he sputtered indignantly. "Don't you know who I am? I'll have your hides for drumheads!"

Byrrah frowned at Tydeus, then looked at Kreeg, who was staring daggers at the Viscount Charybdis. "What—certainly you don't mean that *he*'s involved?"

Tydeus straightened his robes the best he could and moved to approach Byrrah and Kreeg. "My prince! Surely there's been some mistake! These crude ruffians came to my door and practically dragged me from my bed! They claim that you ordered my arrest on grounds of treason!"

Before Byrrah could respond, Kreeg stepped forward, glowering down at the confused Tydeus. "Do you deny the charges?"

Tydeus blinked, more confused than angry. "Of course! It's complete and utter nonsense!"

Byrrah turned to scowl at Kreeg. "I gave no such order for his arrest!"

Kreeg's glare fixed itself on Byrrah and the prince felt his heart shrivel. "Your Highness must be mistaken," he said, his voice as cold and unyielding as volcanic glass.

"Yes. Of course. I *must* be," Byrrah responded weakly.

"Tydeus, after you left the royal palace, did you speak to anyone concerning the plans for Vashti and the others?"

Tydeus's eyes shot around anxiously before settling on his feet. "Well, um, not exactly."

"What do you mean, 'not exactly'?"

"Well, I—um—may have mentioned something to my betrothed."

"Betrothed? I was not aware you were engaged to be married, Tydeus," Kreeg said darkly.

Tydeus's fleshy cheeks darkened slightly. "Well, it's not official yet—I was planning on asking her tomorrow."

"Who is this woman?"

"A distant cousin of mine, the Lady Tethys. Why do you ask?"

"Because a young mermaiden fitting the description of your kinswoman was seen helping Hiordis and Seth escape arrest earlier this evening!"

Tydeus looked genuinely stunned. He blinked and swallowed and turned to face Byrrah. "My prince, there's been some terrible mistake. Tethys would never have done something like that! She's probably still home, innocently asleep in her bed!"

"Sergeant, did you search the Viscount's villa, as I ordered?"

"Yes, Warlord."

"And did you find a young woman in any of the guest chambers?"

"No, sir. All we found were the Viscount and a handful of servants staying in rooms off the scullery."

"I rest my case. Highness, I strongly request that you sign death decrees for the traitors Baron Hiordis, Lord Seth, and the Lady Tethys—"

"No!" Tydeus yelped. "Not her! She's but a girl! Seth and Hiordis must have kidnapped her to use as hostage against me!"

"She ran one of my men through with a harpoon while escaping the city battlements!" Kreeg snapped.

"Enough!" Byrrah sighed, holding up his hand for silence. He turned his attention to Tydeus, who was now trembling like a newborn seal pup. "Your loyalty toward your cousin is commendable, Tydeus. To tell you the truth, I'm surprised by it. Unfortunately, your bride-to-be has left you to stand alone to face treason charges.''

''But, Your Highness—!''

''I've heard enough. Take him to the dungeons.''

* * *

Vashti looked up as the door to his cell opened and Tydeus was unceremoniously booted in.

''As if being confined in this pesthole was not bad enough,'' the old Chamberlain grumbled, ''now I have to share it with the likes of you!''

Tydeus sat on the floor, staring in dull surprise at the manacles on his wrists and ankles. ''I don't understand—there's been some kind of horrible mistake! I don't belong here!''

''Ah, but you *do*,'' Vashti sighed. ''You seem to forget: it is *I* who am wrongly imprisoned. But now you see what becomes of dogfish who would swim with the sharks.''

''It's all Kreeg's fault! He's the one who set me up!''

''I am an old man, and one who has long ago set aside the ways of the warrior for the wisdom of the scholar. But if you do not cease your whining, I swear I will muster what little strength I have left and throttle you with the very chains you and your erstwhile friends have clapped me in! Now be quiet and let me go back to sleep!''

Tydeus fell silent, his lower lip trembling as he rocked back and forth on the dungeon floor. It was all a horrible mistake. A misunderstanding, that was all. And once his prince had come to realize that, he'd send for him, and then the old man would be sorry for treating him so horribly.

* * *

Breakfast found Kreeg waiting for Byrrah in the royal dining room, a sheaf of death decrees in hand. Byrrah cringed inwardly as he seated himself at the head of the table. As if the warlord were not an unpleasant enough sight first thing in the morning, the stack of execution warrants was certainly enough to put a man's appetite at bay.

''Must I deal with this so early?'' Byrrah groaned. ''I haven't even had a chance to down a cup of cod oil.''

''It cannot wait, Highness. Especially now that Hiordis and Seth are at large.''

''I suppose you're right, Kreeg,'' Byrrah sighed, removing his signet ring in order to em-boss the decrees with his personal imprint. "Although, until the Congress officially approves my claim, these warrants are essentially invalid."

"Leave that worry to me, Highness."

Byrrah did not hesitate to stamp his seal of approval onto the death decrees for Hiordis and Seth, and his hand wavered only slightly when it came to the Lady Tethys's name. But the last two warrants made him stop.

"You would have me execute Tydeus and Vashti?"

"Vashti is your enemy. Tydeus is a liability."

"I will not have Vashti executed!" Byrrah barked. "He is far too valuable to be destroyed, simply because you do not trust him! He has served as Chief Chamberlain for over a century. There is much to be learned from him. Besides, he is the most respected elder in the city. To execute him on the grounds of treason would seriously undermine my claim to the throne. If the old fellow should suffer a seizure of some sort or fall ill after my coronation—well, accidents do happen. But I will not sign his execution warrant!"

"As you wish, milord. And Tydeus?"

"I agree, he *is* a liability. His injudiciousness has cost us much. But *death*? Don't you think that's rather harsh? Wouldn't it be just as easy to banish him—?"

Kreeg leaned forward, his fierce gaze pinning Byrrah to his seat. "Tydeus is a fool. But what is even more dangerous: he is a fool with a *big mouth*. He blathered our plans to his cousin—how long do you think it would be before he blathered the truth about Namor to one of our enemies?"

"You're right, Kreeg. He *is* too dangerous to live," Byrrah sighed, and brought his signet down on the death decree bearing Tydeus's name. "The poor fool. He wanted so much to be important."

* * *

When the jailer opened the cell door that morning, Tydeus was certain that Byrrah had experienced a change of heart overnight, just as he'd known he would. But when Kreeg stepped into the dungeon, Tydeus's hope of reprieve dissolved right before his eyes.

"Tydeus, Viscount of Charybdis, you have been found guilty of the charge of treason and sentenced to death by Prince Byrrah, Lord of Atlantis."

To Tydeus's surprise, Vashti spoke up, his aged voice indignant. "Byrrah? That's ridiculous! Byrrah does not yet have the power to sign, must less enforce, such a decree!"

"Silence, old one!" Kreeg snarled, his hand dropping onto the pommel of his sword. "Byrrah insists that you are still of use to him alive, but do not tempt me! As for you, Tydeus, you are to be executed within the hour. I suggest that you use the time to make your peace with Neptune."

After the dungeon door slammed shut behind Kreeg, Tydeus turned to Vashti, his fleshy face now deathly pale. "Vashti, what is the punishment for treason?"

"Do you really want to know?"

Tydeus nodded.

"Death by baiting."

Tydeus winced and grew even paler, but said nothing more. He spent the rest of his allotted hour sitting on the narrow bunk, staring off into nowhere. When the executioners arrived, he stood without being told to do so. As they led him from the cell, he turned and spoke one last time to Vashti.

"Should you get the chance—tell my cousin, the Lady Tethys, that I do not blame her for what she did. She was right. I was the one who was wrong. Tell her I know that now.''

"Yes, Tydeus. I will tell her.''

* * *

The place of execution was a valley located well beyond the walls of the sunken city. A large pillar covered with barnacles and half-eroded hieroglyphs stood in the very center. Heavy wrist chains and ankle chains were set into the face of the baiting block. Although it had been a century or more since the last execution, the pillar and the chains were still stained purple with the blood of past victims. The barbarity of death by baiting was so raw that few of the more recent monarchs of Atlantis had been willing to use it. Namor had never resorted to it. But something told Tydeus that the baiting block was soon going to be seeing a lot of use.

Kreeg was already there, waiting for him. Of course. Kreeg was hardly one to pass up a chance to watch another's suffering.

"Have you any last words, Viscount?'' Kreeg sneered.

"Where is Byrrah? Where is my prince?''

"He elected not to come. It seems Byrrah does not have much of a stomach when it comes to such things as this.''

At Kreeg's signal, the executioners dragged Tydeus down into the valley and chained him, spread-eagle, to the pillar. Tydeus tried to remember the words to the prayer for the dead, but all he could think of was Tethys. Somehow thinking of her made the ritual slashes across his wrists and ankles less painful. If he was lucky, he would bleed to death before the sharks arrived.

As the life seeped from his body into the surrounding sea, Tydeus hoped that wherever his cousin was, she was safe and would remain so. He wished he could tell her how sorry he was. His thoughts of Tethys were interrupted, however, by the first of the hungry shadows, scything its way through the water toward him.

And then there were only screams.

CHAPTER 5

TRAPPED BETWEEN WORLDS

He was somewhere strange.
He was nowhere at all.
He was dead and damned.
He was in Hell.

But it was not the Hell of the air-breathers. The Atlanteans did not have a Heaven as humans understood it. When a noble warrior or honorable citizen died, their spirits went to the Hall of Poseidon, to serve the Great Thunderer as he saw fit. Sometimes he sent the spirits back for rebirth. Sometimes he turned them into Nereids, or undines, or monsters like the Scylla. But those who died in shame, who had done evil deeds, or who had proven themselves unworthy—they were condemned to an eternity within the molten cores of the sea volcanoes that dot the ocean floor. And that's exactly where Namor was.

He had failed in his duty as ruler of Atlantis. He had left his people to the mercies of his enemies. He was damned to spend millennia trapped within a boiling heart of lava, his skin blistered as red as a lobster's. There was no denying where he was—he could feel the relentless heat ravaging his flesh. No matter how hard he tried to get away, his arms and legs refused to move. It was as if he were encased in red-hot jelly that weighed on his limbs like an octopus.

Phantoms emerged from the roiling lava to taunt him. Although he had not seen any of them in years, their faces burned brightly in his mind's eye. There was Nereus, his grandfather, and his mother, Queen Fen. Neither said anything by way of greeting or admonishment, but both shook their heads and scowled disapprovingly. A third figure emerged from the volcano's heart. Unlike Nereus and Fen, the newcomer was human and dressed in the uniform of a merchant marine. Namor was dimly aware that he was looking at his biological father—but try as he might, he could not bring Leonard McKenzie's face into focus.

The faceless father turned to Fen and cocked a thumb at their progeny.

"I don't know why you bothered t'keep him, darlin'. You shoulda put him onna ice floe the moment he were born. Nothin' natural could come from us havin' a kid."

"Mother—" Namor croaked, reaching out to her, but she turned into shadows at his touch.

"Namor—Namor, my sweet husband—"

The Lady Dorma swam out of the lava, her beautiful features composed into the peaceful smile he last saw on her face before she perished in his arms. Even in Hell, he felt his soul cry out for her. He missed her so much. There wasn't a day that went by without his thinking of her. Over the years since her death his grief had muted to a low, persistent ache deep at the core of his soul. Seeing her again caused that ache to flare into sorrow. He tried to reach out to her, but somehow she managed to be just beyond his grip.

"I long to kiss your lips, dear one," Dorma whispered. "But now that can never be, for you are of the Damned. I begged Father Poseidon the boon to see you one last time before you were to be consumed by Hell's molten embrace. Farewell, my prince. Farewell.''

''Dorma—no! Don't leave me, my wife—! I beg you!''

Dorma's blue form wavered, became indistinct, then turned green. In his first wife's place was his second, the alien amphibian Marrina, who had undergone a horrendous mutation while trying to birth his child. It transformed her into a ravaging sea monster that he had been forced to slay himself.

''M-Marrina?''

''How do you like being dead, Namor?'' she sneered. ''Isn't it odd how you can spend your life working for the good of others, putting the welfare of your fellows before your own concerns—only to find yourself condemned for one mistake?''

''Marrina—''

But she was already gone. In her place stood two new figures, both female. The one on the left was the Princess Namora, his dearest friend and beloved first cousin; the one on the right was a human woman dressed in fashions he had not seen since the Second World War. It wasn't until she smiled that he recognized Betty Dean—the first human to befriend him and the first woman he'd ever truly loved. These two, of all the phantoms, did not seem to be angry or disappointed in him. But then, Namora died before he had become ruler, and knew nothing of the dereliction of duty that landed him in Hell. As for Betty Dean—she had always forgiven his transgressions, even when he declared war on the surface world decades ago.

He was the Avenging Son. The prophesied protector who would lift Atlantis up from the shadow-haunted depths and restore her to her place of power amongst the kingdoms of the world.

But he had fallen far short of his promise— he had died and left his people vulnerable to enemies within and without. Atlantis had suffered mightily at the hands of the barbarian reavers and Lemuria's warlords over the centuries. His superior strength was what had kept his kingdom and its outlying settlements safe from their enemies, and had finally tipped the balance of power in Atlantis's favor.

Once the whales sang of his death, the news would travel the currents pole to pole within days. And knowing the Avenging Son to be no more, the foes of Atlantis would be quick to strike. Even as he thought these things, the images of his most persistent arch-enemies shimmered into existence. There was the barbarian Attuma, and the renegade Atlantean warlord Krang, the vicious hybrid freak Tiger Shark, the evil siren Lorelei, and the Lemurian sorceress Llyra, the one responsible for the death of the Lady Dorma. They were all pointing at him and laughing at how he had been made impotent by death.

"Away with you!" Namor screamed, clamping his hands over his ears. "Cease your gloating, blackguards! Be silent, or I swear I shall claw myself free of this damnable prison and crush your laughter with my bare hands!"

Just as his enemies' laughter grew so loud that he was afraid his head would burst, there was a dim, white light and the sound of a familiar, cherished voice speaking as if from a great distance.

"Namor—?"

He lowered his hands from his face and looked up. Hovering above him, as tranquil as a manatee suckling her child, was Susan. She looked as she had when he first saw her, years ago, before her marriage to the leader of the Fantastic Four.

"Namor—" Her voice was closer now,

stronger. "Namor—I want to help you."

There was a sharp pain in his arm, and when he looked again, he could see that Susan was armed with a harpoon, its tip dripping blood. He opened his mouth to cry out, to ask her why she had betrayed him, but as he mouthed the words, he realized that he was no longer burning.

As he succumbed to the darkness nibbling at the edges of his mind, he felt vaguely ashamed that he would have thought Susan capable of such duplicity. She had not betrayed him. She'd delivered him from Hell.

* * *

Sue winced as Reed's voice came in over the communication headset built into her suit's helmet. He was excited, and when he got that way, he tended to talk a little too loudly.

"Sue! How is he? Sue?"

"He tried to fight me, at first. Even in a weakened state, he would have been too much for me to handle. But then he went limp and let me give him the shot. The results were almost immediate. He's resting quietly right now."

"Excellent! I think we've managed to beat Von Doom on this one, sweetheart. Namor's reached the turnaround stage."

"You mean he's going to make it?"

"Yes, darling, he is."

Sue was surprised to find the back of her throat tight. She let out a slow, shaky breath before responding in a low whisper, "Thank God."

* * *

Ben glowered at the sleeping form of the Sub-Mariner as he floated in the isolation chamber, still wired into the diagnostic web. "So, Charley the Tuna here's gonna pull through, huh?"

"All data points to that conclusion," Reed replied over his shoulder, still obsessed with something the computer was working on.

"Good. Feelin' sorry for the gill-man ain't my strong suit. Speakin' of which—why ain't he awake?"

Reed turned from the computer screen to stare directly at the unconscious Sub-Mariner. "I can only hazard an educated guess, Ben. His fever is gone and his lungs are repairing themselves. His vital signs are growing stronger and stronger with every passing hour. I believe he is undergoing a healing process unique to Atlantean biology—falling into a form of suspended animation while his body recuperates."

Ben sighed. "Meaning?"

"He'll wake up when he wakes up."

"Well, thank you, Marcus Welby."

Johnny strolled into the room dressed in a formal tuxedo. He had his hands in his pockets, and he whistled merrily to himself. Ben lifted an eyebrow at the sight of the Human Torch's evening clothes.

"Hey, squirt, why the monkey suit? You got a hot date lined up for tonight?"

"You could say that," Johnny smirked, "if you were a vulgar baboon. But why be redundant?"

"Why you smart-mouthed li'l—!" Ben lunged forward, making a half-hearted grab at Johnny.

Johnny easily sidestepped the Thing and thumbed his nose. "Aww, you're just jealous 'cause *you* don't have a date with Leila Lee!"

The Thing's jaw dropped and his baby blues came close to popping out of their sockets. "Leila Lee? *You* gotta date with Leila Lee?!?"

Johnny tugged on his lapels and cuffs, grinning ear to ear. "I'm picking her up at eight! We're having dinner at Tavern on the Green."

"Ooooh, aren't we the fancy-pants!"

"Yeah, well, *we're* the one on the date with Leila Lee, remember?"

"Don't remind me."

"Excuse me, but exactly who *is* this 'Leila Lee' you both keep mentioning?" asked Reed, looking mildly piqued.

"Aww, man, you'd *have* to be married to ask a question like that!" Johnny laughed. "Reed, where have you been for the last six months? Leila Lee's only the world's top supermodel! She's been on the cover of all the magazines—*Vogue, Cosmopolitan, Elle, Sports Illustrated, Paris Match . . .*"

"Well, I doubt that my being married has anything to do with my ignorance of who she is," Reed chuckled. "Unless she was on the cover of the *Cambridge Review of Physics* or the *Journal of Applied Cybernetics*, I doubt I'd recognize her."

"What I wanna know, hotshot, is how did you end up landin' a date with *the* most lusted-after dame on the face of the Earth?" Ben demanded, prodding Johnny in the chest with a blunt, rocky finger.

"Honestly, Ben!" Johnny rolled his eyes in disgust. "Only *you* would call Leila Lee a 'dame'!"

"And you still ain't answered my question, Sparky."

Johnny's checks reddened slightly and he looked down at his shoes. "Her, uh, publicist set it up."

"Her *what*?"

"Publicist. You see, there's this fashion mag that wants to do a layout featuring super-models and super heroes, and . . ."

"It's a *fashion* shoot?" Ben could not contain his amusement. "Some date! You mean you're goin' to a shoot with her? Sounds really intimate and hot to me!"

Johnny's face turned completely red as he clenched his fists. "The magazine loaned me this tux for the evening, and it's *not* fireproof. But, buddy, you're gonna be in for one hell of a hotfoot when I get home!"

"Ooh! Look at me, I'm all aquiver with fear!"

There was a beeping sound from the computer, and Reed twisted his head one hundred and eighty degrees to look at the screen. What he saw made him spin the rest of his body around in the chair as well.

"It looks like Namor's starting to wake up. I'd better alert Sue. He'll no doubt be severely disoriented . . ."

"You do that, brother-in-law. My thoughts

will be with you as I dine on Oysters Rockefeller tonight.''

''Izzat so?'' Ben called out after Johnny as he left the room. ''Then I'll be thinkin' about you while I'm eating macaroni and cheese.''

* * *

She was the first thing he saw when he opened his eyes.

She was leaning over him, her small hand in his, smiling and repeating his name over and over.

''Susan,'' he whispered. Then he coughed, bringing up a lungful of water and mucus. It was only then that he was aware he was no longer underwater. Panic flashed in his eyes.

''Don't worry—you're okay now. Your lungs are working properly again.''

''I feel—strange,'' he rasped. His vocal chords felt as if they'd been left to dry on a beach.

''It's to be expected,'' she replied soothingly. ''You've been horribly ill. You almost died.''

''Almost?'' He smiled thinly. ''I thought I had.''

Reed Richards's face came into his field of vision. ''Namor—do you remember what happened before you got sick?''

Namor's features hardened, his eyes narrowing to slits. "Byrrah."

Mr. Fantastic and the Invisible Woman exchanged glances.

"Your cousin?" Sue asked gently.

"I—I fell ill while reviewing the troops. Byrrah and his co-conspirator saw to it I was kept from the Royal Physician. They poisoned me somehow. It was Byrrah's plan to replace me as ruler. The fool! He has allied himself with one of my more—unstable—warlords. A cur by the name of Kreeg. Byrrah thinks far too highly of himself, and far too little of Kreeg, to realize the danger he is in. It will be only a matter of time before the warlord's harpoon finds my cousin's heart and the throne falls into his blood-stained hands!''

"Were Byrrah and Kreeg the only ones involved in the plot to assassinate you?"

"I suspect one other: a picayune nobleman by the name of Tydeus. I suspect he duped his cousin, the Lady Tethys, into unwittingly aiding in their plot to poison me. But I still don't understand—my tasters checked everything at the banquet . . .''

"Because you weren't poisoned, at least not

in the traditional sense," Reed explained. "You were slipped what was intended to be a lethal microbe—a virus especially tailored to affect your immune system. It wouldn't have affected your tasters. And if you didn't have literally in-human stamina, those intentions would have been met."

"Such trickery is not beneath my cousin, but the methods are far beyond his reach. The same holds true for Kreeg and Tydeus. You had a rea-son for asking me who else I suspected, Reed Richards. Do you know something concerning this attempt on my life that I do not?"

"The virus was artificially produced. I have reason to believe it was the creation of Dr. Vic-tor Von Doom."

Namor's brow furrowed. "Doom? Doom is behind this?"

"All the evidence points to him," Reed said. "It would seem that your cousin enlisted Doom's help to engineer his coup."

Namor shook his head. "That is impossible, Reed Richards. How would Byrrah contact Doom? Or even know him in the first place? My cousin has never left the cradle of the sea. He speaks and understands no tongue except that of our fathers. Although he is my elder, Byrrah is naive when it comes to the surface world. No, it was Doom who sought out Byrrah, not vice versa.

"Although my cousin detests air-breathers, he is not above using them to suit his own ends. And as I said earlier, he sorely overestimates both his wiles and his intelligence. He gravely erred in his judgment concerning Doom. I can only hope it is not a fatal one."

"We'll have time to figure out Von Doom's role in this later on. Right now the important thing is how you're feeling," Sue said.

"To tell you the truth, I'm famished."

"I'm hardly surprised. You haven't eaten solid food in days. Is there anything in particular you'd like?"

"Raw fish."

"Sashimi it is."

* * *

Namor sat in the middle of the kitchen of Four Freedom's Plaza, wrapped in a mid-calf length terrycloth housecoat, with a cup of green tea at his elbow, making his way through a second sashimi combination platter.

As he chewed a piece of octopus, he was aware of being watched. Without turning to look to see who was there, he lifted the cup of tea to his lips and said, "Susan tells me I owe you my life, Ben Grimm."

"Yeah, well, Suzie's a bit overdramatic, sometimes," the Thing grunted, shambling into the kitchen. He lowered his bulk onto a chair specially designed for him. "Ugh. Beats me how people can eat that stuff! I know it's real trendy—but gimme good ol' steak an' potatoes any day o' the week! Then again, I guess there ain't much in the way of cows or spuds where you're from, is there?"

"Hardly."

Ben twiddled his thumbs for a second, shifting uncomfortably under Namor's gaze. "Reed sez that your cousin was the one who put the whammy on you. I was just wonderin'—I mean, he's family, right? Why would he want to kill you?"

Namor sighed and pushed aside his plate. "I am not entirely certain Byrrah meant to kill me. Perhaps he only meant to incapacitate me. And if I just happened to die along the way—well, that would not grieve him overmuch."

Ben shook his head. "I still don't get it. Sure, my old man boxed my ears more'n once when I was comin' up—and I used t'fight cats 'n' dogs with my cousins—but the moment anyone said anything against the Grimms, we stuck together like glue and gave the devil the hind-most! I'd never lift a hand against family—not even that sleazeball my Aunt Jenny married who drank up the money for her operation!''

''I envy you your familial devotion, Ben Grimm,'' Namor said, his voice suddenly tired. ''Unfortunately, such intrigue is to be expected if one is to be sovereign. It does not help matters that my cousin—amongst others—considers me unfit to rule because I am half-human.''

''I guess bigotry ain't limited to us air-breathers, huh?''

''All my life I have had to deal with such resentment.'' Namor smiled crookedly. ''You seem surprised, Ben Grimm. Do you find it strange that I know what it is like to be reviled for my physical appearance?''

''No, it's just that—well, you don't seem to be hurtin' in the looks department to me.''

A sudden motion at the corner of Ben's eye caught his attention. Johnny was tip-toeing past the open door in the direction of his rooms. Ben got up and quickly nabbed the boy by the scruff of the neck, dragging him into the kitchen.

''Whoa! You're not gettin' off th' hook that easy, Sparky!''

"Put me down!"

"Not before you tell Unca Benjy how your hot date went—uh-oh!"

Ben stared at what was left of Johnny's evening suit. Which wasn't much. The dark blue of his uniform could be seen peeking through his elbows, knees, and the middle of his back. The smell of charred material filled the air.

"What happened t'*you*?" he marveled, lowering the Human Torch.

"What's it look like?" Johnny fumed. "I had a really crappy date!"

"You wanna elaborate on that?"

"Not particularly." Ben fixed him with a stare that indicated that that was the wrong answer, so Johnny sighed, and continued, "Well, I go to pick her up at her apartment, right? But she's not alone. Her photographer's there, and so's her make-up man, and her hairdresser, an' her wardrobe people, and her publicist, *and* her personal handler! So we go to Tavern on the Green, but instead of having dinner there's this buffet table set up on the patio. Before I can get something to eat, the make-up person and hairdresser have to do a number on me. And by the time *they're* through with me, everything on the buffet table's gone except some seedless grapes and baked brie. I *hate* baked brie!''

"Yeah. But what about Leila Lee?''

"I'm *getting* to that! So we start doing the shoot, and Leila won't say two words to me. Instead of talking to me, she talks to her handler, who turns around and repeats everything she says back to me. Then the photographer decides he wants to shoot some pictures of us together riding in the back of one of those hansom cabs that go through Central Park. I say okay. What's the harm, right? So, we're in the cab, and I'm getting kind of up close and personal with Leila, right? And she's starting to finally warm up to me—then I hear this scream and look out of the cab and see this jogger being mugged!

"So I flame on, right? I nab the mugger, pretty as you please, but when I turn around to wave at Leila and bask in the glow of her adoration—the carriage's gone! The photographer and the driver are still there, though. They're lying on the ground. Seems the horse freaked out big time when it saw fire and bolted—with Leila still in the carriage!

"The hansom cab made it out into traffic on Park Avenue—don't ask me how. And, wouldn't you know it, just as I make the scene, *Spider-Man* brings the horse under rein! Leila was all over the lousy wall-crawler like a cheap suit! And—to top things off—I found out there was a mix-up. I wasn't the super hero they wanted for the shoot! They thought I was Thor!''

''Sorry to hear yer dream date went into th' toilet, hot stuff,'' Ben snorted, doing his best to keep a straight face.

''Yeah, I'm drowning in your sympathy.'' Johnny turned to Namor in an attempt to change the subject. ''Uh, so, Namor. I see you're doing better.''

''Yes—thanks to you all.''

''Yeah, well, we're like that, you know. Uh, look, I really need to change outta what's left of this suit.'' With that, he hurried out of the kitchen in the direction of his rooms.

''Poor kid,'' Ben chuckled, sitting back down. ''When's he gonna learn he just ain't cut out for the jet-settin' circuit?''

''You don't know how lucky you are, Ben Grimm,'' Namor said softly as he stood up. ''I envy the closeness your team has, even when you argue amongst yourselves. You are a true family. Treasure that.''

* * *

Namor sat in the diagnostic chair, wires taped to his body and head, and scowled at the readout flashing across the computer screen.

"So—what does your machine say, Reed Richards? Am I well enough to return to Atlantis?"

"You're recuperating at an impressive rate, considering that you were at death's door less than twenty-four hours ago. But as for you being ready to return to Atlantis, I'm afraid that it will be several more days before you're in peak condition again. Although you may feel better *now*, you are still suffering the effects of extreme exhaustion. Odds are, within a half-hour of swimming in open water, you'll become seriously fatigued . . ."

"I can outswim the fastest submarine in your miserable Navy!" Namor snapped. He grabbed the wires and tore them free from his body as if they were paper streamers. "Pfah! I'll tell you what 'fatigues' me—it is all this endless testing and re-testing! I should have known better than to trust surface-world technology!"

Muttering darkly under his breath, the Sub-Mariner stormed out of the lab.

Sue sighed, and said, "I'll bring him back, Reed."

"Thank you, Sue," Reed said. "It's important that I finish this battery of tests to determine if he's in any danger of a relapse."

* * *

She found him on the roof, looking out across the concrete and glass canyons of Manhattan in the direction of the ocean. He seemed so horribly, completely alone with himself that for a moment she was afraid to speak. Namor turned his head slightly in her direction, and glanced at her out of the corner of his eye.

"Are you here because your husband needs me for his experiments? Or do you come to me as a friend, Susan Storm?"

"Can't I have it both ways? And it's Richards, now. You know that."

Namor shrugged and returned his gaze to the water glinting in the distance. "A slip of the tongue."

"Sometimes the mistakes we make tell a lot about ourselves," Sue said, moving to join him at the railing.

"Surely it tells you nothing you do not already know."

"Namor, I want you know that I understand what you're going through—at least part of it, anyway. You're a man of action, a man born to make decisions and determined to have them carried out. I know you're eager to return to Atlantis to settle your score with Byrrah and Kreeg. But you have to be patient. You're still too weak to swim to the bottom of the sea, much less orchestrate a palace coup once you get there!''

Namor sighed and lowered his head. ''My mother always said my pride was my great failing. Perhaps it is because I had to prove myself in the eyes of my subjects. I *know* that what you tell me is true. Although I can feel my strength returning, I am somewhat—hollow. It is as if I am a vessel that has been emptied, and is now slowly being refilled. Part of me burns to return to Atlantis; yet another, wiser, part tells me that to do so now could very well cost me my life. I have just escaped Death's gaping jaws—I have no urge to have it swallow me whole now.''

''Then come back to the lab. It's important that Reed finish the tests.''

''I will do as you say, Susan. But I must confess that I find your mate quite—confusing. I have much respect for his intellectual prowess, but sometimes I feel as if I am no more than a biological curiosity, something for him to poke and prod to satisfy his scientific curiosity.''

''I will admit that Reed's bedside manner is

somewhat lacking. But he's not as cold and distant as you make him out to be.''

''Obviously. Or you would never have come to love him as you do.''

The way he said the words—with a tinge of melancholy and envy—made her look up into his face. Namor's sea-green eyes were regarding her with an openness she'd rarely experienced with any man beside her husband. She quickly looked away.

* * *

''I see Sue has talked you into coming back,'' Reed commented as the Sub-Mariner re-entered the laboratory.

''Your wife can be very—persuasive.'' Namor brandished his right forearm, the inner elbow of which was covered with puncture marks. ''I assume you will require yet more of my blood for your experiments?''

''That won't be necessary this time.'' Reed set aside his stethoscope and turned to regard the Sub-Mariner face to face. ''Namor—have you considered asking a third party to help you regain the throne?''

The Sub-Mariner blinked, somewhat unprepared for Mr. Fantastic's shift in topic. ''What kind of third party?''

"The United Nations."

"I do not see how they could help me to win back my kingdom."

"Namor, the United Nations was established with the purposes of maintaining international peace and security, developing friendly relations among nations on the principle of equal rights and self-determination, and encouraging international cooperation in solving international economic, social, cultural, and humanitarian problems."

Namor folded his arms across his chest. "I am fully aware of the organization's noble and worthy causes, but I still do not see how they might be useful to me. For the ruler of Atlantis to go before a congregation of surface-dwellers and beg for their help? You forget, Reed Richards—I have been before this august body of yours once before, and Atlantis was denied membership. Why should they move to help now?"

"This is vastly different from last time, Namor. You could warn them about what the surface world might expect if Byrrah and this Kreeg you've mentioned were to rule Atlantis. It would be in their interest to see that someone more—moderate—was on the throne. You could even reapply for membership.''

Namor stroked his chin, deep in thought. ''What you say intrigues me, Reed Richards. Perhaps reapplying for membership could serve both me and my kingdom well. The times have changed drastically since my grandsire's days. Thanks to humankind's technological advancements, the ocean is no longer a world unto itself. We Atlanteans pride ourselves on being civilized longer than the surface world, but we have yet to evolve such a diplomatic tool as this. Perhaps it is time for Atlantis to join the modern world, instead of fearing and hating it, as do Byrrah and his co-conspirators.''

''Spoken like a true enlightened despot, Namor,'' Reed grinned.

''I beg your pardon?''

* * *

It was early the next morning when the Thing shambled into the kitchen area in search of his daily pot of coffee. Reed was sitting at the table, the daily newspapers spread about him.

''Did you call in that favor from yer high falutin' political bigwig friends?'' the Thing asked, dumping the contents of the coffee pot into a mug the size of a soup bowl.

''Judge for yourself,'' Reed said, holding up

the front page of the *Daily Bugle*.

" 'Reed Richards to Address UN on Behalf of Sub-Mariner.' Oh, Shamu's just gonna love *that*!"

"I'm well aware how he'll react," Reed sighed, lowering the newspaper. "It's the best I could do. Namor has made many enemies over the years. He's unpopular with those countries that still participate in whaling and intrusive fishing ventures, such as Russia, Norway, and Japan. Plus he's caused a lot of trouble for off-shore rigs over the last few years, which means that all the major oil companies, both privately and publicly owned, consider him an ecological terrorist . . . "

"Yeah, he's a real popular guy, our Subby."

The two fell silent as Namor entered the room. The Sub-Mariner seemed to be in relatively good spirits, his skin having lost the last of its waxy pallor.

"Good morning, Reed Richards, Ben Grimm. What news do you have of my request to address the Assembly?"

Mr. Fantastic and the Thing exchanged looks. Ben shrugged and picked up the sports page. "You're the one who came up with the bright idea, Stretch, not me."

"I'm afraid it's a good news–bad news situation, Namor," Reed explained.

The Sub-Mariner's brow furrowed, his manner suddenly stern. "What do you mean?"

"It means that the General Assembly is interested in hearing your story—but they want me to be the one to address them."

Namor's eyes darkened like a coming storm. "*What*?"

Reed held his hands up in an attempt to defuse the Atlantean's anger. "It seems that several important member-nations have qualms about allowing you in the building, much less addressing the General Assembly. I argued with the American diplomatic committee over this for *hours*! I was finally forced to call a couple of business associates connected with S.H.I.E.L.D. The Secretary-General has agreed to allow me to address the Assembly on your behalf."

The muscles in Namor's jaw were standing out in such relief that their every twitch was visible. He took a deep breath and folded his arms over his chest. "Very well. If that is how it must be, so be it."

"You still feelin' sick, Namor?" the Thing asked, lifting a craggy brow. "It ain't like you to take somethin' like this so—calmly."

"There is more to this than simply my pride, Ben Grimm," Namor replied. "The welfare of my subjects is at stake. I will swallow my anger and ignore this insult. To react violently now is beneath my dignity as sovereign of Atlantis. And I count myself lucky that I have been granted a spokesman of such integrity and intelligence as yourself, Reed Richards."

"You honor me, Namor," Reed said, blushing slightly. "And I will do all in my power not to fail you or your people."

* * *

"I dunno, Reed," Ben grumbled as the limo pulled up to the United Nations Building. The plaza was swarming with newspeople, sightseers, and protestors armed with signs. "Do ya think us showin' up in costume is such a good idea?"

"Probably not as good as leavin' Namor back at Four Freedom's Plaza with Sue," Johnny commented, peering through the tinted windows at the mob outside. "Jeez, he's not exactly popular, is he?"

"You can say that again, hotshot! But looks can be deceivin'. Seems t'me like the oil companies got their goons out in force, pretendin' t'be protestors. Hey—whazzat sign say? 'Just

191

Say No to Monarchy'.''

"It's not *all* anti-Namor, though. Look, there's Greenpeace, Amnesty International, WorldWatch, and Pan-Gaea, too!'' Johnny noted. "They're the ones with 'All God's Children Need Freedom' and 'Mermaids Have Civil Rights, Too'.''

"And there's 'American Legion Outpost #637 Supports Sub-Mariner: WWII Hero!' Hey, Stretch! Mebbe this won't be as bad as we thought!''

Reed shook his head. "I'm more afraid of what's waiting for us on the Assembly floor than outside, Ben. Inside, they're not carrying signs.''

* * *

"Wow, some joint, huh?'' Ben said, his normally garrulous tone hushed to a respectful whisper as he and Johnny were shown to their seats in the V.I.P. gallery overlooking the General Assembly.

"I've seen it on TV and in the movies, but I've never really been here before,'' Johnny replied, looking down at the massive horseshoe-shaped amphitheater. The floor of the General Assembly was a colorful anthill of activity, with cultural attachés and diplomats hurrying back and forth.

"Hey, what are these for?" Ben snatched up a headset and clamped it on. A woman's voice, speaking French, filled his ears. He reached out and carefully spun the dial in front of him. The voice went from German to Spanish to Russian to Japanese to Chinese to Swahili to Tagalog to a language he'd never heard before. "Cool! Now I can listen t' political hogwash in twelve different languages!"

"The Secretary-General is stepping up to the podium, Ben. I think Reed's next!"

"Yeah, well, I hope it goes smoothly, for our sakes," Ben grunted. "I'd hate t'have to punch my way outta this place."

* * *

Back at Four Freedom's Plaza, the Sub-Mariner and the Invisible Woman watched the live broadcast from the General Assembly on the Richardses's fifty-three-inch television in their private quarters.

"You seem a little anxious, Namor."

"I'm afraid I have too much riding on the outcome of your husband's speech to be anything *besides* anxious, Susan," the Atlantean replied with a small smile. "Although I will admit to surprise at the outpouring of sympathies from certain groups of humans."

"You mean the Greenpeace and Pan-Gaea protestors they showed? Namor, I realize your exposure to human society has been somewhat—eclectic. Most of the people you know are like us—or the Avengers or the Defenders. There are plenty of ordinary, everyday humans who fight for what they think is right, without super-powers of any sort. Not every human on the face of the planet thinks that it's right to treat the oceans like a toilet, destroy fragile ecosystems in the name of money, or hunt whales to extinction! For many of these people, you're a symbol of the environment, fighting back against those who would pollute and exploit it. No matter what your people may think or feel about us, humanity is not your enemy. Ignorance is."

"Well spoken, Susan. I only hope your husband can plead my case half as well."

Something on the television caught Sue's eye, and she turned off the mute on the remote control. "Looks like this is it." A wave of applause burst from the speakers as the Secretary-General's face filled the cameras.

"Ladies and gentlemen, esteemed ambassadors, members of the press, and honored guests, it is my pleasure to introduce to the General Assembly a man who has done more for planetary peace than any other scientist this century. I give you Dr. Reed Richards.''

Reed moved toward the podium, looking tall and dignified. Instead of a suit, he wore the trademark blue uniform of the Fantastic Four. Sue couldn't help but smile proudly at the sight of the man she loved standing before the assembled dignitaries of the world.

After bowing his head to accept their applause, Reed cleared his throat and spoke in the strong, booming voice that Sue knew all too well. She personally believed that if Reason were to have a human voice, it would be Reed's.

''Ladies and gentlemen; esteemed ambassadors; it is a great honor for me to stand before you! Many of you first knew me as a scientist and inventor. Other have come to know me through my exploits in the Fantastic Four. I come to you today, not to speak of technological marvels, scientific breakthroughs, or threats to the world by forces from beyond our solar system. Instead, I am here to speak on behalf of another, whose domain lies far closer to home.

''The one whom I am representing is known to many of you here simply as the Sub-Mariner. But I know him as Prince Namor, Lord of Atlantis. I am aware that many of the nations represented here today have grievances against Prince Namor. But I am not here to discuss the rights of Atlantis versus the rights of different sovereign states. I am here to ask your help in the name of peace and international justice.

"As I said, Prince Namor is the sovereign ruler of Atlantis. As such, he is a head of state, due the autonomy and rights inherent to such a title. But I have proof—" Reed held up a thick sheaf of printouts and a set of computer diskettes "—that Prince Namor was the target of covert aggression so devious, so deliberate, and so utterly without mercy, that I do not hesitate in calling its instigator evil! Indeed, I also have reason to believe that the aggression was planned and carried out under the orders of the ruler of an independent state, with the intent of placing a puppet dictator on the throne of Atlantis! And, to make matters even more serious, the aggressor used biochemical weaponry expressly forbidden by the Geneva Convention and roundly condemned by every civilized nation!"

The British ambassador, looking anxious, spoke up. "Dr. Richards, who is this aggressor you mention?"

"None other than Victor Von Doom, the ruler of Latveria."

There was an immediate buzzing amongst the ambassadors and their staffs. The looks on their faces ranged from alarm to outright terror. Victor Von Doom, the iron-clad monarch of one of the tiniest Balkan states, was internationally feared and respected, much the same way that a shark or a cobra is respected. His scientific genius was second only to that of Richards himself, which had brought the two into fierce conflict time and time again since even before the Fantastic Four's founding.

Scowling at the disorder which the mere mention of Von Doom's name had caused, Reed struggled to regain his audience's attention. "I know what some of you must surely be thinking! But let me hasten to assure you, I do not make this charge frivolously. And while I have had numerous clashes with Von Doom over the years, believe me, I am not in the habit of blaming him for every evil that befalls my friends, family, or associates! As I said before, I have concrete proof that a genetically engineered virus, one tailored to attack the immune system of Prince Namor and no other, was patented by a Latverian bioengineering company.

"I do not know what purpose Von Doom has in seeing the Sub-Mariner dead. But I know from personal experience that Von Doom's interests are never to the benefit of anyone but himself. And I also know that, for all the perceived trouble Prince Namor may have caused various whaling companies, commercial fishing fleets, and oil concerns, his attitude toward our people is moderate, compared to those with whom Von Doom would replace him. In fact, how many of you have recently received reports of freighters lost at sea? Ferries mysteriously sinking? Or the inexplicable disappearance of personnel from offshore rigs?"

Again the excited murmurs swept the gallery.

"Although we cannot see what transpires below the waves, the fate of Atlantis is as important to world peace as what transpires in Haiti, Korea, or any other nation. While Prince Namor is, without dispute, one of earth's mightiest mortals, he is but one man. He is now recovering from the assassination attempt that came perilously close to claiming his life. He needs your help in reclaiming his homeland! And, despite a long-standing grievance between *homo mermanus* and *homo sapiens*, I was able to convince him that the United Nations holds the key to solving his dilemma!

"If this august body of diplomats can bravely put aside decades of superstition and prejudice and treat the Atlantean problem as it would any other, Prince Namor is willing to open an embassy here in New York and reapply for membership status. I beg of you to use this chance to show that the people of the surface world are indeed interested in the welfare of those who live on the ocean's floor. Thank you."

Reed stood down from the podium, allowing the Secretary-General to retake the microphone. "We will now hold open discussion on the topic Dr. Richards has brought forward . . ."

Suddenly the picture of the General Assembly was gone, replaced by a housewife wondering how to keep her family's laundry clean and fresh-smelling.

"What's happening? Why did they stop?" Namor asked, perturbed by the sudden shift of gears.

"It's okay, Namor. It's just a commercial. They'll resume broadcasting in just a few minutes. Besides, we'll be the first to know the results."

The housewife with laundry problems was replaced by a young man peddling a car. Then an announcer's voice came on the air.

"We now take you back to our live coverage of Mr. Fantastic's address to the United Nations General Assembly."

A handsome, middle-aged man in a trench coat stood in the plaza outside the U.N., speaking into a portable microphone. Behind him was a seething mob of photographers, newshounds, protestors, and sightseers. "Hello, I'm Nelson Brockman, reporting live from U.N. Plaza, where super-scientist and leader of the Fantastic Four, Mr. Fantastic, has just finished addressing the General Assembly on behalf of the Sub-Mariner. He requested intervention concerning a palace coup believed to have been sponsored by the notorious super-villian, Doctor Doom. I—"

Brockman's face scrunched in on itself as he pressed his finger against his right temple, apparently listening to something coming in over his earpiece.

"Wait a moment, something has happened—I'm not sure exactly what, though—it seems the Fantastic Four are leaving the building—"

The throng of spectators and paparazzi was

sent flying in all directions like duckpins and a familiar voice could be heard bellowing over the din of the crowd.

"Gid outta my way, ya lousy buncha news-hungry vultures!"

Oh no. Please, no. Sue covered her eyes, unwilling to look.

The Thing shouldered his way through the mob as if he was surrounded by bothersome school children, his brow creased and his mouth set into a scowl. All but the most famous—or foolhardy—of reporters fell silent at the sight of him. Brockman regained his composure quickly enough to thrust his microphone into the Thing's angry face.

"Mr. Grimm! Mr. Grimm! Perhaps you can tell us what went on in the General Assembly? Did they make a decision concerning the Sub-Mariner's request for help against Doctor Doom?"

Ben rounded on the reporter, and for one tense moment it looked as if he might punch the camera. "What did they *do?* I'll tell ya what they did, buddy—they didn't do *squat!* The minute they heard Doom was involved they ran fer cover like scared rabbits! Reed's still in there, God bless 'im, tryin' t'talk sense to those yella-bellied creeps! One of those fancy-pants ambassadors got up and said international law could not be extended t'Atlanteans because they weren't human! I had t'get up an' leave t'keep from bustin' up the joint!''

"*Enough!*" Namor brought his fist down on the remote, shattering it. The television went blank. His face was surprisingly controlled, though Sue could see the rage in his eyes as he stalked toward the elevator. The doors hissed open and he entered, Sue trailing behind him.

"Namor, please, there's still a chance Reed can talk them into doing something."

"I have allowed your husband his chance, Susan. He did his best—I cannot fault him for that—but I should have known how it would end! For all its claims to high ideals and love of peace, the United Nations is still composed of surface-dwellers. And no matter how I may feel toward some of them, surface-dwellers cannot be trusted! I was a fool to think otherwise! The fate of Atlantis is mine alone to decide."

The doors hissed open again. They were on the roof. Namor turned to face her one last time, smiling sadly. "I thank you for all that you and your friends have done for me, Susan. And for those things you tried to do. But I have been gone from the game too long. Farewell, Susan Storm.''

Before Sue could correct him, Namor hopped onto the protective railing that lined the observation deck and stepped off into empty air, taking wing in the direction of the East River.

There were any number of ways she could have stopped Namor. She could easily restrain him with a force field—but for how long? Sooner or later, he would have his way. He was ruler of Atlantis, and he always got his way.

Almost always.

She ran downstairs to the hangar. At the very least, she could keep an eye on him, so if he did collapse from exhaustion, she'd be there to help him.

The Fantasti-Car could be separated into four autonomous one-person modules. As Sue prepped one of those modules for takeoff, she punched up her brother's access code on her communication link. The Human Torch's face winked onto the screen.

''Hey, sis—what's up? You catch Reed's speech on the tube?''

''Yes, and we also managed to catch Ben's, too. Namor's gone, Johnny! He flew the coop—literally.''

Johnny slapped his forehead and grimaced. *"D'oh!* Way to go, bricks fer brains!"

"Tell Reed what's happened, but try to be subtle about it. I don't want people thinking Namor's gone off to get even with the surface world. But he's not in any condition to tangle with the likes of Von Doom, either. I'm going to trail him in the Fantasti-Car. The rest of you get back here as soon as you can and catch up in the F-4, okay?"

"I read you loud and clear, big sister! We'll be home as soon as possible!"

Sue gritted her teeth as she lifted the Fantasti-Car module into the Manhattan sky. As she trained the scanners to seek out Namor's unique biological signature, she felt a chill come over her, but she was certain it had nothing to do with the wind whistling past her. She couldn't help think about the way Namor had said goodbye. As though he was certain they'd never meet again.

Well, you don't get off that easy, Namor, she thought. *You're getting our help whether you want it or not.*

CHAPTER 6

THE RETURN
OF THE KING

*I*t felt good to be back.

   As he made his way through the murky depths of the East River, Namor exulted in the sensation of being in his true element. Despite its name, the East River was actually a saltwater channel, albeit a heavily polluted one. Although it reeked of spilled diesel and raw sewage, Namor could taste the sea in his gills. And there was simply something about open water that made his spirits soar and his heart race like a young swain in love. As foul as it was, the pollution of New York Harbor was preferable to the stale, artificially oxygenated water that had filled his sickroom.

He shot past the city's famed docks, narrowly avoiding an underwater welder patching a hole in the Staten Island ferry's underbelly. Namor was nearly a mile away before the welder's brain registered what his eye had glimpsed—a man, naked except for a pair of green swim trunks, moving with the speed of a torpedo.

The pleasure of his return to the sea was almost enough to make him forget the grim fate that certainly awaited him. Almost. But not quite.

* * *

"I hearda guys leavin' inna hurry before, but you'd a thought Subby could have been bothered to use the front door!" Ben quipped, hands on hips. Reed and Johnny were with him, with Sue's face gracing the large communications screen on one wall. Reed was working at a laboratory table on some kind of serum.

"You should talk," said Sue, her voice raised slightly so she could be heard over the heavy wind. "I'll have you know this is partially your fault, Benjamin Grimm! You and your big mouth! You *knew* Namor was watching the news coverage on TV! And you had to go and flap your lips!"

"I'm sorry, Suzie! Honest I am! If they wuz handin' out prizes for lunkheads, I'd take the blue ribbon! But I was so damn mad! And that news jockey caught me off balance—"

"I'm afraid Ben's slip-up merely spurred Namor to act an hour earlier than he would have anyway, that's all," Reed sighed, looking up from his work. He looked both weary and disgusted. "I argued with both the General Assembly and the heads of the Security Council as best I could. Even if they'd agreed to take action, I'm afraid it wouldn't have been what Namor expected or needed."

"Yeah," Johnny added. "What good are economic sanctions against Latveria?"

Sue said, "In the meantime, Namor's heading for Atlantis. He's following the Gulf Stream north. And, Reed—he's swimming much more slowly than he should."

"All right, Sue. The three of us will be along in the F-4 shortly."

"I'll be here," Sue said. Then her face winked out.

Reed looked at his brother-in-law and best friend. "It would seem that *somebody* has decided to help Namor reclaim his throne."

"And who might that be, boss-man?" Ben said with a mock sigh.

"The Fantastic Four."

"Figgers. And me without my water wings."

* * *

The sub-basement of Four Freedom's Plaza was deeper than the subway tunnels, gas mains, electric cables, and sewage pipes of Manhattan. And a good thing, considering that it contained a tunnel linking it directly to the East River.

The F-4 Submersible was a nuclear-powered submarine that accommodated six passengers—seven at a pinch—but was strong enough to withstand the pressures of the Marianas Trench. It sat in its special submarine bay, patiently awaiting its crew.

"I've programmed the F-4 to home in on Sue's Fantasti-Car module," Reed explained, as the trio crawled down the hatch into the belly of the midget submarine. "If we're lucky, we should be able to catch up to her—and to Namor—within an hour or two. By my calculations, he'll begin to tire long before he reaches the mid-Atlantic."

Johnny was the last one in, sealing the hatch. "I programmed the Plaza's in-house security,

Reed, and I grabbed an underwater suit for Sue.''

"Thank you, Johnny," Reed looked up from the F-4's computer. "Get ready, everyone.''

Within seconds the F-4 was making its way out of the submarine pen into the East River. Ben squinted through the shatter-proof bubble at the feculent water, his face twisted in disgust.

"Phew! Willya lookit the filth? An' those twerps inna U.N. complain that fish face is dangerous, when we've gone an' done this to his backyard.''

* * *

Namor began to grow weary about a hundred miles off the coast of Nova Scotia, near Sable Island. Even though he was swimming with the Gulf Stream, his arms and legs were starting to feel leaden. Unaccustomed to such physical infirmity, Namor cursed his weakness and struggled to press on.

There was a sound distorted by the underwater thunder of a nearby offshore oil rig, yet unmistakable to his ears. It was Atlantean speech. Over the millennia the merhuman language had evolved into something completely different from human speech, becoming more and more like the ultrasonic clicking and squealing of dolphins. And, to any human ear monitoring the noises of the sea, there was no telling a pod of porpoises from a cadre of crack Atlantean commandoes. Unless you were an Atlantean yourself, of course.

"Careful, Atheus—"

"Blow us back to Atlantis—"

"Shut up and keep an eye out for air-breathers—"

There were six of them, gathered around one of the rig's barnacle-encrusted support stanchions. He could tell from the design of their livery that they were in Kreeg's employ, not Atlantean regulars. They were outfitted with harpoon guns, nets, and the bioelectric pistols that worked much the same way as an electric eel, discharging a shock strong enough to disable prey or, in this case, drown humans. Judging from their conversation, they were trying to place an explosive device on the rig.

Namor was aghast. He despised the offshore oil platforms as much as any merman, but had Byrrah gone *mad*? The resulting pollution from the crude oil spilling into the surrounding ocean would make the *Exxon Valdez* disaster look minute!

* * *

Atheus muttered darkly as he struggled to activate the magnetic seal that was supposed to couple the device to the surface-dweller's ugly ocean-raping machine. Perhaps it was nervousness that made his fingers seem so heavy and awkward. Once affixed to its target, the bomb would switch over to an automatic sixty-second countdown: barely enough time to get out of the kill radius on their jet-sleds. Personally, he had no taste for such subterfuge, but Sekis had commanded him to do it. And Sekis was the squadron leader, as he was so fond of reminding everyone.

One of the warriors shouted a warning and the water was suddenly driven out of his gills. Something struck him like a Great White snatching up a seal. Atheus's first and only thought was that he had, indeed, been attacked by one of those merciless predators, then he lost consciousness.

* * *

"Atheus has been hit!" one of the younger warriors cried, too startled by the pale blur that had come streaking out of the darkness to register what had attacked them.

"The bomb! Where's the bomb?" yelled Sekis.

"Have no fear, squadron leader! It is in safe hands. As is your companion."

The warriors stared in stunned surprise as Namor floated fifty yards away, holding the bomb aloft in his right hand, the limp body of Atheus draped over his left arm like a discarded robe.

"It's Prince Namor!" gasped the youngest of the warriors, his eyes agog. "But he's supposed to be dead!"

"Byrrah rules now!" snarled Sekis, firing his harpoon gun. "And this pasty-skinned freak is going to be dead *again* in just a couple of seconds!"

Namor dodged the oncoming harpoon, which missed his head by a fraction of an inch. He dropped the unconscious warrior but maintained his hold on the bomb. He could not afford to allow it to fall back into the hands of Kreeg's loyalists. As he swam toward the surface, he heard a muffled cough as a net-launcher fired, then was surrounded by a crackling web of bioelectricity. Normally, he would have torn through the net as if it were seaweed, but the accompanying shock was powerful enough to send him plummeting to the seabed.

"Kill him!" screamed Sekis. "Kill him and get the bomb!"

The young warrior approached the ensnared Sub-Mariner, drawing the traditional tri-pronged Atlantean shortsword known as a shark's tooth from its scabbard. As the warrior prepared to deliver the fatal blow, a blue arm shaped into a lariat looped itself around his neck.

"I'm afraid I can't allow you to do that, young man." The blue arm snapped backward, sending the Sub-Mariner's would-be murderer flying through the icy waters in the general direction of Halifax.

The helmeted head of Reed Richards, perched atop a neck as long and thick as a kraken tentacle and covered in a protective uniform, shot forward, scrutinizing Namor through the net's latticework.

"Are you all right?" he asked, his voice slightly altered by the helmet's speaker.

"I may be winded—but I am far from helpless, Reed Richards," Namor assured him as he tore the net apart. "*Imperius rex!*"

"Now that's th' pointy-eared fish stick I know an' can't stand!" the Thing growled as he emerged from the F-4's airlock.

Sekis's face darkened until it looked like he

would burst a vein. "Air-breathers! In the name of Warlord Kreeg—kill them! Kill them all!"

One of the remaining warriors dove at the orange beast slowly plodding its way toward him, his war-trident ready to pierce the monster's vitals.

"Blasted helmet—can't see a damn thing unless it's right in front of my ever-lovin' nose—!"

"Ben! Look out!" yelled Reed.

The warrior's trident struck the Thing squarely in the chest, and the tines bent back as if made of putty. The warrior gaped at his ruined weapon, then at the glowering orange face staring out at him through the helmet's faceplate.

"Son, I don't know if yer tryin' to kill me or just make me mad. Either way, yer in trouble."

The force of the Thing's backhand blow sent his attacker flying into one of the oil rig's supports hard enough to knock him unconscious.

"Be careful, Grimm!" Namor shouted. "Do not hurt them! Although they may serve my enemy, these are still my subjects!"

"Yeah, I'll keep that in mind the next time one o' yer 'subjects' is tryin' to stick me with a frog-gigger!" Ben grumbled under his breath.

Another warrior tried to make his way into the F-4's open airlock, only to be shot back out as if fired from a cannon. The Invisible Woman emerged from the airlock, pantomiming dusting off her hands.

"And stay out!"

Sekis cursed his luck; this *would* have to happen to him! And after he'd curried Kreeg's favor for months! He'd taken the assignment assuming that he would return to Atlantis covered in glory. Now it looked as if he'd be lucky to return in one piece.

All the combatants, human and Atlantean, froze at the distant trumpeting of a conch shell. Ben turned in the direction of the call and saw two dozen more Atlantean warriors, heavily armed and riding underwater ski-sleds, headed their way.

"Great! Now look who's comin' ta dinner."

Upon sighting the rapidly approaching warriors, Sekis lunged forward and snatched the bomb away from Namor, fumbling with the manual override switch.

"Long live Warlord Kreeg! Long live the reborn Atlantis!"

"Good lord!" Reed exclaimed. "He's triggered the bomb!"

"Since you love air-breathers so much, half-breed, it's only fitting that you die with them!" Sekis spat, hurling the explosive device at the three members of the Fantastic Four.

"I don't think so," the Invisible Woman responded, throwing a force field around the bomb, seconds before it detonated. The force of the blast was funneled upward and away from both the oil rig and the F-4, causing a six-story column of water to shoot straight up into the air. Although some of the wildcatters working the rig's upper decks were doused, there was no real damage done.

"Darn nice shootin', Tex," Ben drawled. "But we still have that cavalry to deal with."

The lead jet-sled came to an abrupt halt about fifty yards from Namor and the others. The rider, dressed in the armor of the Imperial Guard, signaled to the others to follow suit.

The Thing stepped forward to stand beside the Sub-Mariner, his big fists clenching and unclenching.

"Look, Namor—I'll try not to hurt 'em, like you asked. But don't hold me to it, okay?"

The warrior removed her crested war-helm, revealing long hair the color of copper.

"You needn't worry about that, Grimm,"

Namor said, breaking into a slow smile. "I know this warrior."

The Atlantean swam forward, Namor moving to meet him. The warrior hesitated for a moment, as if uncertain whether to believe her eyes, then threw her arms around Namor's broad shoulders in a fond embrace.

Namor scooped his younger cousin up in his arms, swinging her around as he'd done when she was a child.

"It *is* you!" Tethys cried, her voice wobbling between laughter and tears. "Neptune be praised! I knew my cousin was lying! I knew you could not be dead!"

"I am very much alive—thanks to the Fantastic Four," Namor explained, gesturing to the team.

"Say, Namor—who's yer lady friend?" Ben grinned.

Tethys could not help but stare at the strange trio grouped before her. She had never seen humans before, much less ones altered by cosmic rays.

"Fantastic Four? But there are only three of them—and how is it that they speak Atlantean?"

"I'll be more'n happy to explain ourselves to th' lady, Namor. We left ol' Hot Pants back in the sub. His powers don't work so good underwater. And as for knowin' the lingo—well, you can thank Reed's handy-dandy universal translator built into our underwater gear!"

"Ben Grimm, this is my cousin, the Lady Tethys. Although when last I saw her, she wasn't a member of the Royal Guard . . ."

"And I'm still not! And neither are my fellow warriors, anymore. We're members of the rebel resistance, not the Royal Guard."

"A resistance? Then my cousin's rule did not go unopposed?"

"It reeked of conspiracy from the very start! When you were whisked off to Byrrah's retreat, and the Royal Physician was refused permission to see you, tongues began to wag. Kreeg and Byrrah ordered Seth, Hiordis, and Vashti arrested on trumped-up charges. Fierce battles have raged in the streets between Kreeg's legions and those loyal to you.

"In the time since Byrrah assumed the throne, it has become clear that Kreeg is the true and present danger. He is a fierce and bloody-minded savage, little different from the likes of Attuma. Now that he is the war chieftain of Atlantis, his brutality knows no bounds! Those who slighted him in the past have been taken from their homes and thrown into the dungeons! And those who dare to speak out against his actions have been condemned to death. Already their heads begin to decorate the pikes on the city's walls!

"My cousin, Tydeus, was one of their first victims. Kreeg and Byrrah have since announced their plans to declare war on the surface world and to 'purify' the undersea kingdoms by ridding them of such non-Atlanteans as the Lemurians. They have already sent forth several terrorist squads to plant explosive charges on offshore platforms and mine the largest of the surface-dwellers' harbors."

"But tell me," Namor asked, "what of Vashti, Seth, and Hiordis? You said they were arrested . . ."

"Vashti is still locked in the royal dungeon. Kreeg wants to kill him outright, but Byrrah will not permit it. Apparently the old man knows more about the running of the kingdom than Byrrah does, and your cousin is attempting to persuade the old one to accept him as ruler and serve him as he did you."

"He'd have better luck asking the tides to change their ways. Vashti is unswervingly loyal to the House of Poseidon and a stickler for proper rituals and observances. He will never accept Byrrah as his lord. But what of Seth and Hiordis?''

"Both succeeded in escaping Kreeg's men and are working to build an army of those loyal to you. Seth has sent heralds to all the outlying settlements and recruits are pouring in, especially those of mixed Lemurian and Atlantean ancestry. Kreeg's threats of purification have made a lot of citizens nervous. Hiordis is leading a battalion similar to mine, trying to hunt down Kreeg's men before they can start their campaign against the surface-dwellers. That is why we are here—we were tracking Sekis's team, hoping to keep them from destroying the oil rig. Just wait until Seth and the others hear of your return! All of Atlantis shall rise up once they know the Avenging Son is back!''

"Speaking of Sekis, where is the scoundrel?''

"Y'mean th' Mad Bomber?'' Ben asked. "He jumped on one a'them scooters and hightailed it outta here while we were dealin' with his little surprise package.''

Before Namor could respond, he went pale and clutched his abdomen. Struggling not to let Tethys and the others see his pain, he bit his lower lip so deeply it began to bleed.

"Namor?" Sue touched his elbow, her concern evident despite the helmet covering her head. "Reed! Come quickly! Namor, what is it?"

Reed frowned and pulled something resembling a mobile first-aid kit from his utility belt. "This is what I was afraid of—he has stressed himself to the point of collapse." He produced a plastic packet filled with a clear fluid and handed it to Namor. "Bite the end off this and swallow what's inside. It's a serum I succeeded in synthesizing before we left. Combined with your hybrid recuperative abilities, it should counteract the symptoms and boost your immune system."

Namor swallowed the serum, but the fever-gleam did not leave his eyes. "So Sekis is making his way back to his master. Soon Kreeg and Byrrah will know that there is no place under the waves they can hide from the Avenging Son!"

* * *

It was supposed to be better than this.

Byrrah stood on the balcony of the royal palace and glowered down at the Great Plaza. Every day, since his grandfather made Namor his heir, he had dreamed of ruling Atlantis. And in all those dreams, the streets of the city were full of happy, cheering crowds, dressed in their finest festival robes, crying his name and toasting his life and happiness. But now he was king and the streets of the city were all but deserted, the doors and windows shuttered, the citizens lurking fearfully in the shadows like minnows hiding in the coral. No doubt the growing number of severed heads decorating the city's gates had something to do with the population's dire spirits.

And it was all Kreeg's fault.

He had always mistrusted Kreeg, but now he was fearful of him. Byrrah did not have a tenth of the trained warriors and mercenaries Kreeg commanded as warlord. Indeed, since the entire Imperial Guard surrendered its commission in protest over Hiordis being named an enemy of the state, Kreeg's men were the only armed forces to be found in Atlantis.

Kreeg's abuse of power as Byrrah's appointed War Chieftain was frightening, even to Byrrah. But he did not dare say anything for fear of finding himself flopping like a sunfish on the tip of Kreeg's harpoon. The warlord needed to keep Byrrah alive for a while in order to legitimize his own standing. The Atlantean Army might tolerate a suspect member of the royal family taking the throne, but a claim from an usurper would trigger full-fledged civil war. As it was, the rebel forces headed by Seth and Hiordis were causing more problems than they should. Byrrah planned to make his own strike against Kreeg long before the warlord had the time to cement himself into the power structure. He had no intention of joining poor, pompous Tydeus above the city gate if he could help it.

"Y-Your Highness?"

Byrrah turned to glare at the young page cowering at his elbow. "What is it, boy? Can't you see I'm busy?"

"W-War Chieftain Kreeg requests an immediate audience with Your Highness."

"I have no desire to speak to War Chieftain Kreeg right now! Tell him to come back tomorrow!"

"B-but—!"

"Are you *questioning* me, boy?"

The page bowed dutifully, although he could not hide the fear in his eyes. "As you command, sir."

Ten seconds later there was a mighty crash as Kreeg kicked open the doors of the Royal Audience Chamber. The page chased after him, his face a rictus of terror. "But War Chieftain! His Highness asked not to be disturbed!"

"Out of my way, boy!" Kreeg bellowed, cuffing the page so hard he sent the boy flying. "Or next time you'll find yourself missing your tongue!"

"Kreeg! What is the meaning of this interruption?!?" Byrrah snapped, trying to sound as authoritative as possible.

"You want meaning?" Kreeg unhooked something from his belt and tossed it toward Byrrah. It was a net—as it floated closer to Byrrah, the prince saw that it contained the head of Sekis, one of Kreeg's lieutenants.

Byrrah swallowed and grew pale, looking away from the grisly trophy. "What has this to do with anything?"

"Not five minutes ago Sekis returned from his mission to the Sable Island offshore oil platform. He told me that not only had he failed to demolish the air-breathers' ocean-raper, but that all of his men were captured!"

"Captured? By whom?"

"Namor and a group of strange looking air-breathers!"

"*Namor*? My cousin is *alive*?"

"Would Sekis tell such a lie, knowing I

would take his head as the messenger of bad news?''

"What are we to do, Kreeg? The moment Namor's return is known, the people will rise against us!"

"What care have I for those fools?" Kreeg spat, shaking his harpoon. "That they had but one heart I could spear and be done with them! If there is to be battle in the streets of Atlantis, so be it! I'll take on the half-breed face to face, and laugh as I ram my barb into his vitals! It makes no difference whether I win or lose, because my forces are already in New York City Harbor! Today is the first day of war against the surface world!"

Byrrah stared at his second-in-command, stunned by this revelation. "War against the surface—? Kreeg, have you gone *mad*? I thought we agreed that we would wait until we had pacified the Lemurians before taking on the surface world!"

"*I* agreed to nothing, Byrrah! You seem to forget who introduced you to our benefactor in the first place!"

"But we had an arrangement! I am your ruler!"

"The only arrangement I have is with

Doom! I do not *serve* you, Byrrah. I merely *tolerate* you! Now, if you would bid me leave, I wish to sharpen my harpoon to celebrate the return of your cousin.''

Byrrah stood and watched, open-mouthed, as Kreeg strode from the room, swatting Sekis's head out of the way as if it was a child's toy. The self-proclaimed Lord of Atlantis lowered himself onto the throne he had so long coveted and allowed his head to drop into his trembling hands.

It was supposed to be better than this.

CHAPTER 7

THE BATTLE
FOR NEW YORK

"**H**ow can surface-dwellers stand to live with such filth?" whispered one of the shock troops, peering up through the polluted waters of New York Harbor.

"If this is how the water looks, imagine what the land must be like!" muttered his comrade-in-arms.

"Silence! No talking in the ranks!" snapped the sergeant, sharply rapping the warrior's gill-helmets with the butt of his war lance. "The commander is addressing the troops!"

"Men, I want to speak to you one last time! Most of you know that this amounts to a suicide mission! It is our job to see to it that all ships anchored in this harbor are destroyed and that the fuel dumps lining the docks are also demolished! Even as we strike against the surface-dwellers of New York City, similar attacks are under way in London, Sydney, Hong Kong, and San Francisco! The time has come for Atlantis to declare herself the sworn enemy of humankind! We shall die as heroes and take our place in the Great Hall of Father Poseidon! Onward, my brothers! For the greater glory of Atlantis!"

"*For Atlantis*!"

* * *

Gary and Delores Wegmann were from Ohio. Every year they took their vacation somewhere within the continental United States. Delores occasionally tried to talk Gary into going somewhere more exotic, like the Bahamas or Mexico or even England, but Gary always nixed it. "See America first!" was how he always ended the discussion. So, over the twenty-four years of their marriage, they had seen twenty states of the Union, some more than once. Now it was New York City's turn as the Wegmanns's vacation mecca.

So far they'd done the Empire State Building, Rockefeller Center, FAO Schwartz, Central Park, and the American Museum of Natural History. Today they were planning on spending a few hours at the Statue of Liberty, then dining somewhere in Chinatown before returning to their midtown hotel. They were standing in line with other tourists at the Battery Park dock, waiting for the next ferry to Liberty Island. Like a good number of his fellow tourists, Gary planned to record the visit to Lady Liberty with his minicam.

"Gary! Get some pictures of the birds, Gary!" Delores said, waving excitedly at the seagulls soaring in and out of the harbor.

"They're called gulls, Delores! And keep your shirt on! I'm gettin' 'em! I'm gettin' 'em!" Gary sighed as he tracked one of the seabirds, following it with his camera as it swooped down to snatch a piece of pretzel Delores had thrown onto the oily waters.

The scummy surface was disrupted by a sudden explosion of bubbles, like those from an air tank, and the seagull screamed and flew off.

"What the hell?" Gary muttered. Even though he was from Ohio, he knew no sane person would be skin-diving in these busy, dirty waters.

An Atlantean soldier broke through the water like a weird deep-sea diver-in-reverse, his spiked helmet full of water instead of air. Delores caught a glimpse of the invader's blue skin behind the face mask and shrieked just like the frightened gull.

"Gary! Look! *Monsters*!"

The soldier grabbed the mooring post closest to him and began pulling himself out of the water. As he backed away from the strange, blue-skinned invader, Gary suddenly realized he was still videotaping, the minicam glued to his eye.

The Atlantean warrior hesitated for a moment, as taken aback by Gary's appearance as he was by his. Then he raised his spear gun and leveled it at the tourist.

"Gary! Put down the damn camera!" Delores screamed, pulling at her husband's shirttail. "It thinks it's a weapon!"

A curtain of fire abruptly fell between the Wegmanns and the Atlantean warrior. Stunned, Gary and Delores looked up to see what appeared to be a young man made out of flame hovering above their heads.

"*Everybody clear the docks! Please, everybody clear the docks! This is an emergency!*" the Human Torch yelled, trying to make himself heard over the screams of the frightened tourists.

"You heard the fireman," Delores said,

dragging her husband away from the action. "And next year, I don't care *what* you say— we're goin' to Cancun!''

* * *

Satisfied the majority of the innocent bystanders had cleared the area, Johnny Storm aimed a fireball at another group of Atlantean troops clambering onto the docks. It was a good thing that Reed sent him back to patrol the harbor for Kreeg's minions, since he wasn't much use underwater, cooped up in the F-4. Still, it was up to him to hold the fort until the others got back, or until some other super-team, like the Avengers, made the scene. Hell, right now he'd settle for help from Daredevil or Spider-Man. There were dozens of the suckers! More than he could possibly contain. And if that wasn't headache enough, he had to be extra careful with his flame, since the wharves were lined with fuel pumps for the fleet of ferries that carried tourists and commuters out to Liberty, Ellis, and Staten islands. One mistake and Battery Park would disappear in a firestorm that would make Dresden look like a campfire.

Meanwhile, underwater, the Human Torch's arrival had not gone unnoticed.

"Commander, there is a burning man flying

in the sky, pouring fire upon us!'' Likon reported.

The war captain nodded sagely. ''Warlord Kreeg warned me of such a creature. Break out the cannon.''

As the Human Torch swooped down low over the surface of the water, scanning the area for signs of activity, an Atlantean warrior bobbed to the surface directly below him, balancing something that resembled a cross between a conch shell and a bazooka on his shoulder. And it was aimed directly at the Torch. Before Johnny could react, a powerful geyser of water struck him with the force of a firehose, dousing his flame and knocking him from the sky and into the harbor.

The Atlanteans were on him in seconds; one threw a weighted net over the struggling human, while another drew his war-trident, ready to pierce his captive's heart and lungs with one motion.

''Time to die, air-breather!''

There was a meaty *thwupp!*, and the sneer faded from the trident-wielder's face. A two-foot-long barbed spear now sprouted from between his eyes. Johnny glimpsed a blue-skinned woman dressed in battle armor behind him, brandishing a deep-sea spear gun.

"For Atlantis! For Namor!" she cried.

The warrior who was holding the Torch captive in his net was genuinely surprised by the arrival of opposing forces, and was even more surprised when Johnny rammed an elbow into the faceplate of his gill-helmet, sending his life-sustaining water gushing out. The shock trooper gasped like a landed fish and let go of the net, diving back underwater. Johnny felt a momentary rush of relief, only to have it almost immediately replaced by panic, as he realized that the net was dragging him down as well.

The spear gun–toting warrior shot forward with the speed of a dolphin, slicing away the net with a dagger kept tucked in her belt, and dragged the drowning human toward the shore. She boosted him onto a nearby dock and returned to the battle without saying a word.

Although it looked like the battle was no longer quite so one-sided, the Torch knew it was far from over. The warrior-woman's troops were experienced fighters, but they were hopelessly outnumbered. It would take more than their bravery and self-sacrifice to win the day.

Still groggy from the concussion from the water cannon, Johnny closed his eyes and focused his concentration and energy inward, mentally rekindling the furnace at the core of his being.

one—

He could feel it beginning.

two—

It always started as a spark, deep inside his belly.

three—

Then there came that wild, panicky knowledge at the back of his head that told him that if he fully embraced the power within him, it would consume him utterly. It was like being at the top of a roller coaster ride, at the very moment before the car plummets downward and the ground comes rushing up to greet you, with a mixture of fear and exultation filling your gut until you scream with laughter.

"Flame on!"

Johnny Storm shot straight up into the sky like a phoenix reborn from its own ashes, the fire that enveloped his body blazing even brighter than before. He swooped down, skimming the surface of the harbor like a low-flying comet, causing the shock troopers to pull back. What he was about to do was exceptionally dangerous, but he was secure enough in his abilities to take the risk. Using his power to control and redistribute heat, he carefully ignited a portion of the diesel fuel floating atop the harbor's waters, manipulating it in such a way that it surrounded the invading Atlanteans. As he hovered above them, his concentration tightly focused in order to keep the flames from spreading any farther, he then began to steadily raise the temperature of the water within the burning ring of fire, causing it to bubble.

The war captain and his second-in-command exchanged looks, then tossed aside their weapons. It was one thing to bravely fall in battle, but still another to meet your ancestors looking like a lobster. The Human Torch reabsorbed the fire and heat back into himself and the waters instantly cooled, allowing the warrior-woman's troops to surge forward and capture their enemies.

Johnny alighted on a nearby dock and waved at the warrior-woman who had saved his life. She swam up to the docks, eyeing him cautiously. With her copper-colored tresses, blue skin, and big brown eyes, the Atlantean warrior-woman was the living embodiment of the mermaids whom generations of lonely sailors had drowned trying to kiss.

"I wanted to thank you for saving my life. But I don't even know your name!"

"I am the Lady Tethys. How is it you speak my language?"

Johnny smiled and pulled a tiny device out of his right ear. It resembled an arcane hearing aid. "I'm wearing a personal universal translator. One of the benefits of being in the Fantastic Four."

Tethys frowned. "You are the air-breather called 'Hot Pants' who was in the machine?"

Johnny blushed and coughed into his fist, making a mental note to fry the Thing's butt next time he saw him. "Yeah. Except my name isn't Hot Pants. It's the Human Torch. I was sent back home to protect the city while the others help the Sub-Mariner."

"Are all air-breathers like you?"

"Oh, no, we—"

"Good," Tethys responded, pushing away from the dock, regarding Johnny much the same way a cat does a large, friendly, but potentially dangerous, dog. "I mean no offense, as you are indeed a brave warrior, Human Torch. But you make me nervous. Fire is a thing of legend for my people, a scourge visited upon us during the days of the Great Cataclysm. I thank you for your help, but it is time my troops and I returned to Atlantis.''

"Yeah, well, I was just wondering if you were doing anything later—?''

"You are indeed a strange man, Human Torch. Fare thee well.''

With that, Tethys sank below the surface of the water, leaving nothing but a trail of bubbles in her wake.

Johnny sighed. *First he strikes out with a super-model, now an Atlantean! Who said being a super hero improved your love life? He'd be better off in a rock band.*

* * *

Byrrah sat on the throne of his forefathers, trying to figure a way out of the gilded deathtrap he'd unwittingly built for himself, the spiked crown resting uneasily on his brow. He didn't bother to glance up when Kreeg entered.

"Byrrah, I would speak with you.''

"What about, Kreeg?'' he sighed, too dispirited to sound angry.

"It concerns the old barnacle in the dungeon.''

Byrrah lifted his head to look at the warlord, frowning slightly. "Vashti? What about him?''

"I want him tortured.''

A flash of anger sparked in Byrrah's eyes. "Vashti is under my protection! We've gone over that time and again, Kreeg!"

"He is withholding important information!"

"Information important to whom?"

"To *me*," growled Dr. Doom, stepping out from the shadows.

"What knowledge could Vashti possess that would be of any interest to such as you?" Byrrah asked.

"You are not incorrect to puzzle that question, Prince Byrrah. Indeed, what information could an elderly courtier impart to Von Doom, the greatest scientific genius the world has ever known? However, science is far from my sole interest.

"I am of gypsy blood. My father was a healer; my beloved mother burned at the stake for being a witch. In the years since her death, I have acquired many books of arcane lore. One such tome dates back to before the sinking of Atlantis. And it was this ancient grimorie that sparked my interest in your drowned kingdom, pathetic as it may be!"

"How dare you speak of Atlantis in such a way!" Byrrah sputtered.

Doom moved surprisingly fast for a man unaccustomed to being underwater. He grabbed Byrrah by the collar of his tunic and shook him so hard the crown on his head toppled onto the floor. "I dare *all*, princeling! For I am *Doom*! And you would do well to remember that, if you would keep life in your body!"

Byrrah fell away from the Latverian monarch, his face flushed navy blue with anger and shame. No one had dared touch him or speak to him that way since his father's death, decades ago. He knew he should summon the guards and order Doom killed for defiling the Royal Person in such a crude manner, but he held his tongue. Something told him that wouldn't be a good idea.

"Why do you think I offered my service in disposing of your accursed cousin, Byrrah? It certainly wasn't because I thought you would make a better ruler! I did it because I wanted something that you can give me! And now the time has come for me to be paid in full."

"Something that I can give you? I don't understand—?"

"I desire the fabled Net of Oceanus and the Trident of Poseidon."

Byrrah tried to hide the look of shock on his face as he spoke. "What you ask is impossible!

243

The Net and the Trident are fables! Old wives' tales and nothing more! If you wish to be paid for the services you have rendered, Von Doom, then demand gold or other riches—at least name something that exists!''

''You can't fool me, Atlantean! I know you lie! Kreeg has informed me that the Net and the Trident *do* exist! Indeed, it was he who promised them to me in the first place!''

Byrrah was stunned. It was one thing to plot the murder of the rightful prince of the realm, but to surrender the most sacred of Atlantean icons to the hands of a surface-dweller was blasphemy! He was so deeply appalled that his fear of the warlord disappeared. He turned to face Kreeg, his eyes gleaming with indignant rage.

''How *dare* you!?! How *dare* you use such holy treasures to bargain with an air-breather! Crabs take your eyes, Kreeg! The Net and the Trident, along with the Horn of Triton, are the foundation on which the royal family was built! Have you no shame?''

''Don't waste your words on me, Byrrah! The Net and Trident are mere trinkets your ancestors used to gull my forefathers into believing you descended from the gods! It matters little to me that some surface-dweller wants to add them to his collection. Just do as you're told and sign the document ordering Vashti's torture. I'll get the site where the damned things are kept out of the old sea turtle.''

''You idiot! Vashti knows nothing of where they're kept. Only members of the royal family are privy to such information. And I will *never* divulge it to the likes of you.''

Doom turned toward Kreeg. It was impossible to read his mood, but it was obvious that he was not well pleased.

''You said there would be no problem in securing the relics. But now I see you promised something you had no ability to deliver.''

''You call me a cheat?'' snarled Kreeg, his hands tightening on his harpoon.

''I call you worse than a cheat—you are a fool! You dream of becoming king, but your vision is even narrower than Byrrah's,'' Doom said. ''You're no more than a bloody-minded peasant—just like Stalin and a host of others I've watched rise and fall over the years. You may have strength and animal cunning, Warlord, but such are not the things royalty is made of.''

''No one speaks to me in such a voice and lives to tell of it!'' the warlord bellowed, his face darkening with anger. "Certainly not a surface-dweller!" He lunged at Doom, his harpoon at the ready. Even though Doom wore metal body armor, the harpoon-master was powerful enough, and his weapon certainly sharp enough, to gore the Latverian like a young harp seal.

Doom turned aside and brought the edge of his right hand down on the harpoon's shaft, shattering it as if it were no more than a toy. Doom's left hand closed on Kreeg's throat, his metal-clad fingers digging into the warlord's exposed gill slits. The Latverian pulled the warlord forward so that Kreeg's nose touched his faceplate. When he spoke, his voice was little more than a whisper.

"And no one attempts to kill Dr. Doom and lives to tell of it!"

A powerful surge of electricity traveled from Doom's hand into Kreeg's body, literally boiling him alive from the inside out. When Doom let go, Kreeg's body bobbed up and down like a piece of flotsam, his arms and legs drawn in on themselves. Byrrah stared in stunned horror at his second-in-command's carcass.

"Thus is the fate of all who would raise their hand against me," Doom intoned, turning his attention back to Byrrah. "Tell me where the

Net and Trident are, little prince, or you will join your co-conspirators in death.''

Byrrah had lived his whole life desiring nothing but to rule Atlantis. He had schemed and planned and plotted his way to the throne, only to find the crown a dreary weight. He knew he had been a bad ruler. He had been weak and allowed his subjects to fall victim to Kreeg's savagery. Byrrah had always lacked courage, even as a boy. It was that tragic flaw, more than anything else, that had decided his grandfather in Namor's favor. That was why Byrrah was surprised to find that the threat of imminent death meant so little to him at that moment.

He was being given a chance to redeem himself. He might have yielded to Kreeg, but he was damned if he would deliver up the holy treasures of his forefathers to the likes of Doom.

''Kill me if you must, but I will not betray my heritage! The things you desire are more than mere symbols—they are relics, gifts made to the first kings of Atlantis by the gods who fathered them. They possess power beyond the comprehension of mortal man.''

''I am aware of their divine origins, Byrrah. That is why I want them. Do you think I traveled to the bottom of the sea simply for some barnacled-encrusted family heirlooms?''

''All the more reason for me to die with my secret, then.''

Doom regarded Byrrah for a long moment, and something resembling respect flickered in the dictator's eyes. ''You mean it. You would rather die than tell me what I wish to know. The blood of kings *does* run in your veins, after all. Very well, if I cannot force your hand by threats against yourself—then I shall threaten the one thing a true ruler values above all else.''

Doom reached inside his green cape and withdrew a tiny vial. A vial that looked all too familiar to Byrrah.

''Ah, I see you recognize what I hold in my hand! However, it is not the same virus I designed to poison your cousin. No, this one is far more inclusive. This one was designed to affect the immune systems of *all* Atlanteans, not just one. And, unlike the one that Namor swallowed, it does not have to be ingested. No, this one, like the virus that inspired it, is airborne. Or should I say, waterborne? In any case, I estimate its kill ratio to be ninety percent. That means that for every ten subjects who breathe it, nine will die. Perhaps more.''

''Monster!''

"I am not a monster, princeling. I am Doom. And Doom always gets what he desires. So what will it be, Byrrah? Do you betray your heritage, or do I wipe out every man, woman, and child of Atlantean birth? The decision is yours!"

"Damn you to the deepest chasm, Doom," Byrrah rasped, his lips trembling. "Very well! The place you seek is called the Valley of the Drowned Gods . . ."

* * *

Von Doom could not help but chuckle as he climbed back inside his one-man submersible. Manipulating deluded, power-hungry fools such as Kreeg, Tydeus, and Byrrah was child's play for one such as himself; something to keep him entertained on dull afternoons. Now it was time to claim his prize. Gifts made by the gods were known to be tokens of great power. To think of all the things he could have accomplished if *he* had possessed the shield of Athena, the helmet of Hades, and the sandals of Hermes, instead of that fool, Perseus!

Well, he would soon rectify such oversights. And then the world would quake at the very mention of the name Doom!

As the submersible sped in the direction of the Valley of the Drowned Gods, Doom caught

249

a glimpse of what looked to be a vast school of fish headed toward the walls of Atlantis. Then an all-too-familiar flash of blue and orange caught his eye.

It was that ambulatory brickyard, the Thing! Closer inspection revealed the presence of the brute's traveling companion, Doom's arch-enemy, Reed Richards, and the cursed Invisible Woman. He did not spot the insufferable Human Torch accompanying them, although he did spy what looked to be the Sub-Mariner, alive and well. Damn the Fantastic Four! Leave it to them to interfere with what had promised to be a rel-atively simple mission!

The very thought of Reed Richards was enough to make Doom grind his teeth to their roots. Richards had proven to be the bane of his existence since they first met at State University, years ago. Doom had been accustomed to being the smartest student in all his classes—smarter than even the tenured physics professors. It had galled him to discover that Richards was hound-ing his heels on the dean's list. No matter how hard he tried, Doom always found himself shar-ing honors with that fool!

The crowning insult came on the night when Doom returned from the library, only to find

Richards puzzling over the diagrams for a device he'd designed that would take its occupant into the fifth dimension. The dolt had the audacity to suggest his equations were incorrect! Doom told the jabbering fool to mind his own business and proceeded with his experiment. A few nights later, instead of traveling into the fifth dimension, the machine blew up, sending Doom to the hospital, scarring him for life. In a travesty of "American" justice, he was kicked off campus for engaging in "dangerous and unapproved experimentation," while Richards went on to graduate with the highest honors in the school's history!

Disgraced, mutilated, and embittered, Doom turned his back on science and embraced the darker arts, as had his mother before him. He traveled to the far Himalayas in search of an ancient order of monks he had heard rumors of. They found him near their mountain retreat, half-dead from exposure, and took him in. Within two years it was *they* who called *him* "Master." After he had learned all they could teach him, he decided to return to his native Latveria—but not as Victor Von Doom, the orphan son of a gypsy witch and a humble healer, but as something far more fearsome.

The monks fashioned a suit of armor for him and placed upon his ruined face a mask of iron, fresh from the smith's forge. At the moment the white-hot metal touched his unprotected flesh, Victor Von Doom disappeared, leaving only Dr. Doom in his place.

Upon returning to Latveria, Doom learned that his homeland was still under the control of the pathetic tin-pot dictator, King Rudolpho. Within a matter of months the old king was dead and Doom was on the throne, having taken the title of "Baron." Neither the Americans nor the Soviets approved of his coup, but none dared raise a hand to stop him. Even back then, Latveria was the tiniest and most heavily armed country in the world. His subjects, numbed by centuries of abuse by their rulers, embraced Doom as a benevolent ruler.

And so it had gone over the years, until he found himself confronting, yet again, his old schoolmate, Reed Richards. Like himself, Richards had undergone a change both strange and irreversible, the result of one of his experiments gone awry. In the years since Richards became the leader of the Fantastic Four, he and his bothersome friends had managed to remain a thorn in Doom's side. Time and time again, Richards had somehow thwarted his plans for world domination. Once they had even conspired to depose Doom, leaving Latveria in the inept hands of Rudolpho's brother, Zorba. But Doom had eventually regained his birthright—ironically with the help of the selfsame foursome; even the imbecilic Thing eventually acknowledged Doom's rule superior to the corrupt ministrations of Zorba.

Still, the Fantastic Four had an annoying habit of escaping the most final of deathtraps, and had a tedious knack for showing up when they were least expected—or wanted.

Like right now.

* * *

Ben gunned the throttle of the Atlantean jet-sled he'd liberated from one of Kreeg's warriors. The engine strained for a long second before shifting gears.

An eighty-year-old grandma in a swan boat could outdrag me in this thing, he grumbled to himself. Even underwater, his bulk was proving a handicap. Swimming was virtually impossible—he had the aquatic ability of a ton of bricks—and if he didn't want to plod after the others on foot, he was going to have to get the hang of the damned machine.

Reed had sent Johnny back to New York in the F-4 to keep an eye on the waterfront, in case Byrrah and Kreeg's troopers decided to start trouble there. To tell the truth, Ben would have been much happier defending his old stomping grounds rather than being a part of the army now "marching" on Atlantis. As it was, he was seriously overburdening the sled, so much so that he was close to dead last in the procession.

Well, at least we're in spitting distance of Atlantis. Ben pressed his stubby forefinger against the stud on his helmet that activated the communications link between his suit and those of the other members of the team.

"Better get your shoes on, kids, we're at Grandma's house! Hey, Stretch! What kind of battle plan have you got up that mile-long sleeve of yours?"

A squeal of static filled Ben's ears, causing him to wince and switch off the audio. Damn! That last fish cake must have whacked his helmet a lot harder than he thought! Great, not only was he stuck at the butt-end of the Easter Parade, he was effectively cut off from Reed and Sue! Talk about suckin' gym socks through a straw—

A movement at the corner of his eye caught his attention. At first he thought it was some

kind of weird deep-sea fish, then he saw it was
a small one-man sub. And if his baby blues
weren't deceiving him, that was the Latverian
royal insignia painted in gold on its side.

The Thing hesitated for only the fraction of
a heartbeat. He knew there was no way he could
get Reed's attention or catch up with the main
body in time to tell them what he'd seen. And
he knew from long experience that wherever
Doom was, trouble wasn't far away.

As he pointed the sled in the direction the
submersible had taken, Ben Grimm could only
hope that he was tracking the lion to its den, and
not following the Devil into Hell.

CHAPTER 8

DEEP-SEA DOOM

The searchlight mounted atop the tiny sub pierced darkness no natural light had touched in millennia. The Valley of the Drowned Gods lay several miles to the south of the ancient walls of Atlantis. In the days before the Great Cataclysm, it had served as the burial site for the island continent's kings and queens. Huge statues dedicated to the ocean and water gods that were so important to the Atlanteans were erected to protect the royal tombs. During the Cataclysm, however, the mighty statues had toppled and the valley had turned into an undersea grotto.

Although thousands of years had gone by

since, the valley was still an awesome sight to behold, with demolished statues the size of sky-scrapers lying on their sides, their faces rendered even more unearthly by the barnacles that spread across them like leprosy.

The remains of the graven images of Poseidon the Earth-Shaker, Oceanus the All-Embracing, Triton the Surf-Maker, Neptune the Fisher-King, and Proteus the Ever-Changing lay sprawled about the valley floor.

Doom, however, ignored these wonders and focused his attention on locating the shrine Byrrah had described to him. It was there he would find the relics he so hungered for.

As his searchlight swept the craggy walls of the valley, there was a glimmer of silver and gold, as bright and fleeting as fish scales. Doom brought the submersible to a halt. Within minutes he was out of the airlock and making his way toward the reliquary.

Despite the importance of the objects enshrined there, the monument was surprisingly austere, like the Shinto shrines of Japan. The jawbone of some great sea beast—possibly one of the prehistoric megalodons that once ruled the seas, had been turned into a toothy arch, under which rested the fabled Net, Trident, and Horn.

The Net of Oceanus lay folded atop a small altar carved from living coral. It looked to be woven from pure silver, with diamonds, rubies, bloodstones, emeralds, and sapphires the size of a human fist serving as weights. A chain of gold dangled from one of the dagger-sized shark's teeth, attached to which was the Horn of Triton—a large conch shell with inlays of silver, gold, and ivory. But the grandest of the treasures was the Trident of Poseidon.

Standing as tall as a man and as thick as a woman's arm, the three-pronged golden lance was rammed, points-first, into the rocky ground, much like the legendary Excalibur once stood in the stone.

If Doom had been merely interested in the relics for their monetary value, he would have found himself richer than the dreams of Croesus. Indeed, the Trident, once melted down, would provide enough gold buillon to provide for Latveria for the next century. But Victor Von Doom was interested in far more than mere money. What charm could riches hold for one as wealthy as himself? No, gold was good for one thing and one thing only—helping him further his plans for conquest.

It was power that fueled Doom's fantasies,

power that stoked his dreams. If what he had read in the ancient texts was true, the mystic energy locked within these ancient relics was awaiting one like himself: a man who knew the old ways—and who was unafraid to use them.

However, the scrolls had made references only to the Net and the Trident as being of any significance and made no mention of the Horn. No matter. He had to act quickly before Richards and his team discovered what he was up to and tried to stop him.

The Net looked easy enough to remove, but the Trident appeared to be somewhat formidable. Mustering his strength, Doom stepped forward and seized the Trident's shaft with both hands, straining to pull it free. The Trident was incredibly heavy, and although Doom's body armor gave him the strength of twenty, it took some doing before he succeeded in budging the relic. There was a shuddering beneath his metal-shod feet, as if a key had turned in a rusty lock, and the Trident of Poseidon suddenly came free.

Staggering under the weight of the oversized fishing spear, Doom turned toward his submersible. It would be difficult maneuvering the relic through the airlock, but it could be done. It *would* be done. For was he not Doom? And for

Doom, there were no impossibilities, only certainties.

However, he was not prepared to find his way blocked by a large, rocky orange gargoyle outfitted in a diving helmet.

"You goin' somewheres with that pig-sticker, laughin' boy?"

* * *

"All hail Namor! Long live the king! Long live the king!"

The water vibrated with the cheers of a thousand citizens as Namor, the Fantastic Four, and the resistance fighters swept through the streets of Atlantis. Tethys and many of the other groups had returned from their missions successful in preventing Kreeg's warriors from starting a war with the surface, and now Namor led an army home. Entire families spilled out of their homes and into the marketplace to welcome their resurrected ruler.

The moment Kreeg's men caught sight of Namor heading the advancing forces, they fled the battlements in disarray. Lord Seth's men quickly rounded them up, shackling them at the wrist and ankle until their fate could be decided.

Sue gave a choked cry of disgust as she espied the heads mounted on the pikes lining the main gate. Next to her, Reed winced.

Namor regarded the grisly trophies, his eyes as hard and sharp as a knife. "Kreeg is no better than the barbarians that sack our outlying provinces! I knew all these men—and all but one were loyal subjects. And even Tydeus, who so sorely abused my good will, I would not have seen treated so basely!"

Tethys stood beside Namor, her voice tight as she squeezed her kinsman's arm. "Tydeus was a fool and a traitor, my prince. But he was my cousin, and he did shelter me in his home. Although he used me as a pawn in his scheme against you, as his closest living kinswoman I must beg your forgiveness and ask that his mortal remains be treated with the respect due a Lord of the Realm."

"Have no fear, Tethys," Namor assured her, patting her hand. "What is left of Tydeus shall be given its proper funerary rites. Unlike Kreeg, I have no taste for humiliating my enemies after their deaths. But I can no longer contain my outrage at such brutish cruelty. Come! There will be time enough for victory celebrations and triumph processions. To the palace!"

With that, Namor shot straight up, over the heads of his joyful subjects, and swam toward the royal palace, rocketing through the water like a guided missile.

As he swam over the Grand Plaza, he could see Kreeg's minions scattering in every direction, their weapons lying where they'd dropped them. The palace coup had turned into a rout, with the usurper's forces abandoning their leader for the safety of the outer provinces. The anger he felt toward his enemies burned in his chest like the molten heart of a volcano. He was uncertain how to handle Byrrah, but he knew exactly what would happen to Kreeg once he laid hands on the bloodthirsty warlord.

He dove toward the balcony that overlooked the Grand Plaza, touching down inside the royal chamber. To his surprise, there were no guards to be found in the room. Byrrah sat by himself on the coral throne, resting his chin in his hands as he stared at the crown and scepter resting at his feet. Uncertain whether he was entering a trap, Namor approached his cousin cautiously.

"Byrrah—?"

Byrrah glanced up at the Sub-Mariner, a look of relief flickering in his eyes. "Good! You're home!"

"Where is Kreeg?"

"Over there." Byrrah pointed to the warlord's body floating lifelessly in the corner. Small fish were already starting to nibble at his fingers.

"Poor Kreeg," Byrrah sighed. "He had great ambition, but not much sense. He was convinced he was the largest shark in the water. But there are far larger—and deadlier—fish in the sea."

"Who—?"

"The metal-clad surface-dweller. The one who calls himself Doom."

"Doom is in Atlantis?"

"Was. He's gone now. As will we all be, soon."

"Where did he go? Tell me, Byrrah!" snarled Namor.

"To the Valley of the Drowned Gods to claim the Trident and the Net."

"He *what*—?!?" Namor grabbed his cousin by the collar, holding him so that their noses all but touched. "You gave him the Trident and the Net?!?"

The sight of his cousin's rage seemed to shake Byrrah from his fugue. "It's not what you're thinking, Namor! He knew about them already—he demanded them as payment for his services! When I refused to tell him where they were hidden, he killed Kreeg right before my eyes and then threatened to infect all Atlantis with the same disease he used on you! What was I to do? The man's completely and utterly mad! I had no choice, Namor!''

"If Doom succeeds in removing the Trident from the shrine, it won't matter whether Doom's handmade germ wipes out every merhuman under the waves!''

"I'm sorry for the evil I've done you, Namor! Truly! I swear upon our grandfather's bones!''

"I'll deal with you later, Byrrah!'' Namor spat, tossing aside his cousin so that he fell sprawled across the steps to the throne. "Assuming there *is* a later!''

As the Sub-Mariner turned to leave, Seth, Mr. Fantastic, and the Invisible Woman entered the throne room.

"Your Highness, the palace is secure. Atlantis is yours once more!'' Seth reported.

"As it should be! See that Vashti is freed from the dungeon. Place Byrrah under immediate arrest! But make sure no harm befalls him until my return.''

"Sir, where are you going?''

"To prevent the end of the world, my friend—at least that is what I hope!"

* * *

The butt of the Trident caught the Thing in the pit of the stomach, driving him into what had once been a statue dedicated to the god Proteus. A normal opponent would have been reduced to a bag of ruptured organs and shattered bones, but all it did was knock the wind out of him.

Doom stepped back, letting the heavy Trident drop, as the Thing got back on his splayed, four-toed feet.

"That's a mighty impressive batterin' ram you got there, Doomsy. I wonder if you'll be as fond of it after I shove it down yer ever-lovin' throat!"

"Always the vulgarian, eh, Grimm?"

"Hey—go with what y'know, I always say."

The Thing's right fist connected with Doom's armored midsection, and although the seawater dragged his punch, it was still solid enough to send his foe flying into the valley wall. Boulders loosened by the impact bounced down onto the Thing, who shrugged them off as if they were pebbles.

"I don't know what yer doin' stealin' Subby's oversized salad-fork, but something tells me it ain't for the betterment of mankind! Y'know, I'm actually glad you showed up, Doomsy! I wuz gettin' sick of playin' patty-cake with those fish sticks! At least I don't have t'worry about pullin' my punches with *you*! Now I can get down t'some serious clobberin'!''

"You scrofulous cretin! I have better things to do than to waste my time trading blows—or insults—with you!'' Doom snarled, pointing his left forefinger at the Thing.

Something struck Ben square between the eyes, dropping him like a bull in a stockyard. It was as if someone had whacked him with the world's largest hammer. Doom stepped forward, rolling Ben over onto his back with a kick of his metal boots.

"You rely on your muscles far too much, Grimm! It left you open to a concentrated sonic blast! Now prepare to greet death!''

As Doom readied his death blow, there was a rumbling so deep it was as if the very earth was groaning in protest.

"What in seven hells—?'' Doom muttered. The ground beneath his feet began to buckle and lurch. "Seaquake!''

Debris crashed into the valley, and as Doom

watched, helpless, a boulder the size of a city bus landed on his submersible, crushing it like a tin can. He cursed his luck as he struggled to free himself from the landslide.

"What is going on? There isn't an active fault for hundreds of miles!"

The Thing was on his feet, sneering at Doom. "Looks like yer one-man sub is sunk, metalhead! That's what y'get fer orderin' things outta the back of funny books!"

"I'm sure you think your ceaseless twaddle passes for wit, Grimm," Doom retorted. "But as far as I'm concerned, it's long since lost its novelty!"

"Sticks and stones, Doomsy."

"Grimm, you unmitigated fool, don't you understand? Something's not right!"

"Yeah, an' I'm lookin' at it!"

A second, stronger tremor shook the valley, this time opening a fissure in the valley floor large enough to swallow the disabled submersible.

"Whoa, Nelly!" Ben yelped, leaping to avoid the widening chasm. Now he was almost nose to nose with Doom, who lifted a hand to stay his enemy's raised fist.

"Grimm, much as I loathe to speak these

words, I feel I have no other recourse; I believe it would be in our best interests if we refrained from our duel and focused our attentions on preventing our mutually assured destruction.''

"Cripes, yer as bad as Reed! What th' hell are you jawin' about, rivethead?''

"I'm telling you we have bigger things to worry about," Doom replied, pointing in the direction of the creature that was uncoiling from the hole in the ocean floor.

Ben's first impression was that it was some kind of snake, writhing in the darkness of a subterranean burrow. Its body was oily and black and looked to be a hundred yards long. At its narrowest point it was as big around as a horse.

But it wasn't until the beast's back arched and it raised its head that he realized he'd been looking at the tail.

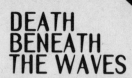

CHAPTER 9

DEATH
BENEATH
THE WAVES

The Leviathan blinked eyes the size of a man and opened a mouth that could swallow a blue whale whole, giving voice to a cry unheard since the days of the megalodon. It had been a long, long time since the Leviathan was last awake.

Doom acted immediately, letting loose with an energy blast from his gauntlets. The creature ignored the blast, trumpeted a call to its mate, and flicked one of its fins, sending Doom tumbling toward the Thing, knocking him to the ground.

"There was enough power in that energy-blast to kill a dozen herds of African bull elephants! It acted as if it didn't even feel it!'' Doom rasped in amazement as he picked himself up.

The Leviathan forced even more of its bulk from the hibernation chamber. Now twice as much of it was visible, and Ben had a sneaking suspicion it wasn't half-finished coming out yet.

''This overgrown guppy's gonna bury us alive without even knowin' we're here!'' Ben yelled. ''And if it's all th' same to you, Doom, I intend to at least go down fightin'! Awright, Reptilicus—*it's clobberin' time!*''

Ben charged the sea creature, fists raised and teeth clenched. He hammered pile-driver blows capable of demolishing diesel trains upon its rubbery hide. The Leviathan issued a low, throbbing grunt and shuddered. It suddenly realized it was hungry. Ben backed away, keeping one eye on the Leviathan and one on Doom.

''Uh-oh. I don't like the way tall, dark, and prehistoric is givin' us the eye.''

The Leviathan struck faster than a snake, its huge head darting forward to snap its monstrous jaws shut on the hapless duo.

* * *

It had been decades since Namor had been in the Valley of the Drowned Gods. The last time was in the company of his grandfather, King Nereus. The old king had brought him there to show him the holy relics and tell him the legend connected to them.

Millennia ago, while Atlantis was recovering from the Great Cataclysm, the undersea kingdom found itself being attacked by all manner of strange beasts. But the fiercest and most dangerous of the sea serpents that plagued them was the one known as the Leviathan. So monstrous was this beast, it alone was rumored to have been responsible for the Great Cataclysm.

The founding father of Namor's line begged Poseidon, his biological father, for help in defeating Leviathan. So Poseidon gave him the Trident, the Net of Oceanus, and the Horn of Triton to first conquer and then bind the great serpent. From that time on, it had been the responsibility of the royal family to make sure that the Leviathan never again escaped its hibernation chamber. That was why the sacred relics were enshrined so far from Atlantis, and their whereabouts known only to the king and his appointed heirs. It would not do to have them exposed to the risk of theft. He only prayed to Father Poseidon that he was not too late.

Namor grimaced, clapping his hands to his

pointed ears, as he was caught in what felt like the aftershock of a depth charge. Although the sound was unlike anything he'd ever heard before, he knew his prayers had been too late. The Leviathan had risen.

As he entered the Valley of the Drowned Gods he saw the vast bulk of the sea serpent as it snapped its gargantuan jaws shut on Ben Grimm and Doctor Doom.

"By Poseidon's beard," Namor whispered between clenched teeth. "I shall see to it that Benjamin Grimm's sacrifice was not in vain!"

Leviathan swung its wide, flat head in his direction, fixing him with eyes that had seen the last of the dinosaurs die trying to crawl their way back to the sea. Namor scanned the valley floor, looking for the shrine that once stood there. The seaquake had altered the terrain, making it almost unrecognizable.

There was a glint of something silvery amidst the debris. But first he had to get past the monster's formidable jaws. The Leviathan made a strange, almost querulous sound, and the sea serpent's mouth began to open, but not because it was about to snap its jaws shut on Namor. Whatever was opening the creature's jaws was doing it from the *inside*.

* * *

The Thing gritted his teeth and shoved harder against the roof of the monster's mouth. Doom lay sprawled beside him, looking dazed.

"I know I'm gonna hate myself for this in th' mornin', but I gotta say it: get outta here, Doom! I can't hold Godzilla's chompers open forever!"

The Latverian monarch did not have to be told twice. Doom scrambled free of the monster's gaping maw, using the jets in his boots to jet himself out of harm's way.

Just as Ben began to feel his grip beginning to give way, he glimpsed Namor rooting about in the rubble of the shrine. Then, with a triumphant cry, the Atlantean held aloft a jeweled conch.

"Hey, Subby! Y'think you could hold off on th' scavenger hunt long enough t'help me out here?" he yelled.

In way of reply, Namor placed the Horn of Triton to his lips and blew a single, reverberating note.

The Leviathan made a noise like a whale hiccuping and Ben found himself speeding into the side of a sea mount with the velocity of a human cannonball. As he rebounded onto the valley floor, he reflected on the good luck of wearing super-thick, rocklike skin. Then again, if he hadn't been wearing the super-strong rock-like skin, he probably wouldn't have found himself being eaten by a prehistoric sea serpent in the first place.

The Leviathan's vast bulk swayed back and forth, like a cobra under the charm of a fakir's flute, and begin to coil back in upon itself, slithering back into the subterranean chamber that had been its resting place for countless centuries. As Ben watched in awe, he realized that his supposition had been correct: it was still only half-way out of its nest. He shuddered to think how big the damned thing *really* was.

The Sub-Mariner moved to help him up from where he'd fallen, a relieved smile on his normally taciturn face.

"I am glad to see you alive and well, Ben Grimm! Not many mortals can tell of escaping the jaws of the Leviathan! You are indeed a fit heir to the ancient heroes!"

"Yeah, well, I owe it all to clean livin'. But we ain't outta th' woods yet, Subby! Where's Doc Doom? If I know him, he ain't gonna let something like nearly bein' eaten alive by a sea monster keep him from what he came for!"

A sonic disruptor blast struck the two, knocking them off their feet. Doom moved forward to stand over them, glowering contemptuously at his fallen foes. "How right you are, Grimm! Doom will not be denied! I came here in search of the Trident of Poseidon and the Net of Oceanus. I will still claim the Trident as my own! And nothing will stop me—not the Fantastic Four, not a sea serpent, and certainly not a half-breed mer-man!"

Namor delivered a solid kick to Doom's chest, sending him flying into one of the toppled gods that littered the valley floor.

"You may be a ruler of men on the surface, Doom," Namor snarled, wiping a trickle of blood from the corner of his mouth. "But here I rule supreme! And as such, I expect—no, *demand*—respect from all who would visit my domain!"

"Yeah, Doom—your butt is grass, and you're looking at the lawn mowers!" Ben grinned, punching his left hand with his right fist.

Namor leaped forward. "Victor Von Doom, you have invoked the wrath of the Avenging Son! Now have at thee!"

Namor and Doom collided with the force of

freight trains, pummeling one another with their closed fists. Although Doom's eyes were slits of hate, Namor's shone with the fire of a man possessed by righteous anger. He had been robbed of his vengeance against Kreeg, and unable to bring himself to visit upon Byrrah the punishment he so richly deserved, but now he was faced with the author of all the misery that had been inflicted on himself, his friends, and his subjects—and he intended to make Doom pay with his life.

Namor's fists connected with Doom's breastplate and facemask, denting metal that could take a mortar round at close quarters without a scratch. Doom seemed unprepared for the fury of the Sub-Mariner's attack. No doubt he was used to either battling opponents physically weaker than himself or, in the case of foes such as the Thing, hampered by "civilized" moral codes that kept them in check. Namor, however, was not pulling his punches. After several poundings, the armor started to sputter. Doom fell to the ocean floor.

"You are right, Doom. I *am* a 'half-breed mer-man'," Namor said, smiling without humor. "And my strength is great enough to survive the ocean depths." Namor grabbed Doom by his cowl, yanking him upright. "You are a loathsome creature, Von Doom! You are lower than a sea slug, and as deserving of kindness!"

"You fool! You think you've won, haven't you? You've won nothing! In fact, you've lost everything!"

"Rant all you like! You're wasting what little breath is left to you, Doom!"

"No one gets the best of Von Doom—no one!" Doom gasped as he reached into the recesses of his cape. "You've condemned not only yourself, but your entire race to death everlasting, merman!" The look of triumph in Doom's eyes flickered as he continued to grope, without success, for the vial containing the virus.

"Lookin' for something, Doomsy?" Ben asked.

"No!" Doom gasped. "The container must have fallen out when the sea serpent—"

"So, the killer microbe you threatened Byrrah with is now resting in the gullet of the Leviathan! How fitting an end for both you and your evil scheme!" Namor laughed, shaking Doom so hard he rattled. With his free hand he bent his index and middle fingers into hooks. "If you have a god, Doom, I suggest you make what peace you can with it."

Ben frowned and stepped forward. "Hey, wait a minute, Namor—whaddaya doin'?"

"I'm going to make Doom pay for all he's done. And the price is death!"

"Whoa, Subby! Nobody could ever accuse me of bein' Doom's Number One Fan, but maybe you oughta chill for a second—"

"Stay back, Ben Grimm! You helped save my life, and it would grieve me to raise my hand in anger against you! But I will not tolerate your interference in this matter!"

"*Namor! No!*"

Namor blinked in surprise. "Susan?"

Speeding toward them on one of the Atlantean jet-sleds was Susan Richards, her husband at her side. A second sled, carrying Vashti and Tethys, was right behind them, followed by the F-4, with Johnny Storm at the helm. Sue leapt from the lead sled and swam toward the Sub-Mariner.

"Namor, don't do it! Don't kill him!"

The Sub-Mariner frowned, confused by her distress. "You would beg for the life of Doom? Your sworn enemy?"

"I realize that what he's done to you and your people is inexcusable, but you mustn't kill him! To do so would make you as bad as he is!''

"Sue's right, Namor," Reed said. "You're no murderer! Hand him over to us! We'll take him back to New York and see that he stands trial in the World Court at the Hague and pays for what he's done!''

Namor grimaced. "More of your precious surface justice! The rulers of your world could not even agree if I was guaranteed the same rights as those of humans! What makes you think they will be willing to dispense justice against those who have wronged me?''

"I don't know. I wish I could say otherwise, Namor, but I can't. The system we humans have is far from perfect—but it's better than what came before. You pride yourself on being the ruler of earth's oldest civilization—but now you're about to kill a man in cold blood!''

"You speak prettily of justice, Reed Richards. And if we were on the surface, perhaps I could be persuaded to heed your words. However, we are not in your world—we are in mine! To you, justice is but a process of law. But it is far more than simply that; it is a rectitude of the soul, enlivened by grace! I am the Avenging Son—and vengeance is mine and mine alone!''

With that, and before any of the Fantastic Four could stop him, Namor hooked his fingers into the eye-slits of Doom's mask and yanked. The mask came away with a sound like a boat running aground on a reef. But instead of revealing a mass of scar tissue, what stared out from behind Doom's iron mask was an elaborate mass of circuitry, synthetics, and a pair of artificial eyes that looked both menacing and vulnerable.

"What treachery is this?" demanded Namor.

"Well, if that don't beat all!" Ben yelped. "It's one of Doom's lousy android doubles!"

"Of course it's an android, you cretinous ape!" Doom's voice crackled from a speaker buried somewhere in the android's head. "Do you think I would be foolish enough to risk myself on the ocean's floor? I had my drone approach that pompous fool, Tydeus, and his bloodthirsty cohort, Kreeg! I thought by providing their insipid conspiracy with some minor assistance, I could eliminate the Sub-Mariner without any real effort. Mark my words, Namor of Atlantis! You may think you have beaten me—but you have signed your death warrant! I shall see you dead—perhaps not today! But some time, when you least expect it, Doom shall be waiting for you!''

''Bold words from a man too cowardly to speak them in the flesh!'' Namor snarled in return, kicking the robot in disgust.

Weird electronic laughter hiccuped from the damaged droid. ''Idiot! While you passed sentence on a robot, Doom has armed this construct for self-destruct! No one gets the better of Doom, mer-man! No one!''

''Not hardly,'' Sue growled, snatching up the disabled android with one of her force fields and hurling it away. Within seconds the robot exploded, and though the force of the blast was contained, the noise it made was loud enough to send the already weakened side of the valley crashing down on the handful of Atlantean and human adventurers below. But the Invisible Woman had been easily able to protect them with a second force field.

''Sheeesh!'' Ben said, clucking his tongue in reproach. ''Talk about yer sore losers!''

CHAPTER 10

FAREWELL TO THE FOUR

It was one of the greatest celebrations the citizens of Atlantis had ever known.

Gathered in the Great Plaza outside the royal palace were hundreds of happy, laughing, cheering merpeople, dressed in their finest festival robes. Scantily clad dancers circled overhead, trailing colored streamers as they performed intricate water ballets, scattering brightly dyed starfish and sand dollars onto the crowd below. Children rode their fathers' shoulders, clutching gaily colored swim bladders tethered to strands of plaited seaweed. Musicians coaxed songs from their instruments, playing tunes that were ancient before the fall of Troy.

In the middle of the Great Plaza stood a raised dais, topped by a throne. It was from this observation point that Prince Namor of Atlantis looked out upon the festival in his honor and found it good. As he watched his subjects dance and laugh and toast his health, the Sub-Mariner felt a surge of pride to know that these were his people. And, praise be to Poseidon, they were alive and well. And he had the Fantastic Four to thank for that.

The quartet of adventurers was clustered together near the foot of the podium. Atlantean etiquette did not allow them to join him on the dais, but they did not seem to take it as a slight. Indeed, they seemed fascinated by the exotic display before them.

"What do you make of Atlantis, my friends?" Reed asked. "Isn't it fascinating how their culture and technology adapted and evolved to their environment?"

"Yeah, it's really something, Reed! But I was thinking how it's too bad we can't take off these helmets and party with these guys," Johnny commented. "I could go for some munchies and something to drink right about now!"

"I hear ya talkin', hotshot," Ben grunted.

"However, I ain't too sure what passes for grub 'n' grog down here is my idea of good eats. Looks to me like they eat a lotta raw octopus an' shark—not to mention their wine's made outta sea grapes an' their whiskey looks like cod liver oil."

Johnny made a face and shuddered. "I think I can hold out until we get topside, if that's the case."

"Hey, Hot Pants—check out Namor's cousin!" Ben nudged him in the ribs, pointing in the direction of Tethys, who was occasionally stealing glances at the Human Torch. "She's really givin' you the ol' fish eye! No pun intended," Ben chuckled.

"Quit it, Ben!" Johnny hissed, blushing bright red.

"She's kinda cute, for a mermaid. G'wan—why don't ya ask her t'dance?"

"Ben!" Sue chided. "You're embarrassing him!"

"I'm not embarrassin' the boy—I'm encouragin' him!"

"I dunno, Ben—she acted real weird when we first met. I think she's scared of me . . ."

"She's never seen a guy burst into flame before, that's all! Besides, she looks like she's gettin' over it. G'wan, kiddo! Kick up yer heels! It ain't every day ya get to save New York City *and* Atlantis!''

A smile spread across Johnny's face. ''You know, Ben—you're right! I think I *will* ask her to dance!''

''Attaboy!'' Ben laughed, clapping the Human Torch on the back. ''Go git 'er, tiger!''

The first few steps Johnny took were bold and strong, but the closer he got to Tethys the more shaky he felt. He tried to cough into his fist to clear his throat, but his helmet was in the way.

''Uh—Tethys? Hi, remember me?''

''You are Human Torch, the fire warrior,'' Tethys responded brightly, turning on the most dazzling smile Johnny had ever seen.

''Uh, yeah. But you can call me Johnny.''

''Jon-Nee?''

''I was wondering if you'd like to dance—?''

Tethys smiled again, but this time she was the one blushing. ''I would be honored, Jon-Nee.''

''You will?'' Johnny had to fight to keep his jaw from dropping as Tethys offered him her hand.

As they prepared to step into the swirling

circle of dancers, a man's voice called out Tethys's name.

The mermaid halted in midstep, looking
about eagerly. "Hiordis?"

Johnny heard the expectant lilt in her voice
and rolled his eyes. Shot down again.

Tethys rushed to greet the tall, powerfully
built warrior with long green hair and the black
patch covering his left eye, still dressed in the
formal battle gear of the Royal Guard. She threw
her arms around his neck and the two embraced
passionately.

"Hiordis! I was afraid you'd been killed!"

"It was a close call—we caught them trying
to mine the Thames waterway! Kreeg's men put
up a fight, but we won out! I only just now arrived! Imagine my joy to see Namor alive and
well and to find you unharmed! This is a great
day for Atlantis!" Hiordis looked up, his eye
blinking as he saw Johnny for the first time.
"Tethys—what are you doing with a surface-
dweller?"

"He is not *just* a surface-dweller, my love!"
Tethys explained. "This is Jon-Nee, the fire warrior known as the Human Torch. He and his
companions helped rescue Namor and liberate
Atlantis from its oppressors. We fought beside

one another in New York City's harbor, and he saved my life. Jon-Nee, this is my beloved, Hiordis, Captain of the Royal Guard.''

"I thank you for saving my beloved, Human Torch. I owe you a debt of honor.''

"That's okay, cap'n. Uh, it looks to me like you two have a lot to catch up on, so I'll just, uh, bow out. Nice meeting you.''

Johnny rejoined the Thing, trying his best not to look too crestfallen.

"So she had a boyfriend, huh, junior?''

"Yeah,'' Johnny sighed. "Skunked again.''

"Chin up, kiddo! There are plenty of other mermaids in the sea.''

The crowd fell silent as the royal trumpeter sounded a long, low note on his conch. Everyone turned expectantly toward the dais in the middle of the Plaza. Vashti, the elderly Chief Chamberlain, stood beside Namor, along with a young page carrying the crown.

Vashti held up a wrinkled hand and spoke with a voice surprisingly strong for one so ancient. "Citizens of Atlantis and honored guests, it is my great pleasure to declare the reign of Byrrah the Usurper at an end! And, according to the custom of our forefathers, I will now publicly acknowledge the new ruler of Atlantis!''

Namor knelt before the old man, his head bowed, as Vashti took the golden crown and held it in trembling hands.

"Namor, son of Fen, grandson of Nereus, in the name of the Great Poseidon from whose loins your ancestors did spring, I crown you king of Atlantis, now and forever." Vashti lowered the crown onto the Sub-Mariner's regal brow. "Arise, Namor I, Ruler of Atlantis, Lord of the Seven Seas! Arise and greet your people!"

"Long live Prince Namor! Long live the Avenging Son!"

Namor held up a hand for silence and the cheers died away raggedly. "Citizens of Atlantis! No prince born has known such brave and noble subjects as you! You have suffered much in my absence, and I will never forget the loyalty and devotion shown by you! But this victory is not mine alone—I share it with many courageous friends. First of which are the Fantastic Four—who came to my aid when I needed it most, and placed themselves in danger for the sake of both myself and my kingdom. And I especially wish to thank Reed Richards, whose wisdom not only saved my life, but who solved the mystery as to who was truly behind the conspiracy against me! He has been kind enough to volunteer his time and resources to devising a vaccine to inoculate all Atlanteans against the virus created by the villainous Doctor Doom, in case he should try and retaliate against us!

"I also wish to thank Benjamin Grimm for his bravery in the face of certain death and for acting to protect relics held sacred to our race since the days of the Great Cataclysm. Without his help, I would have surely perished and the Trident of Poseidon would have been lost to us forever! I also owe much to Susan Richards, lovely and gracious wife of Reed, who pulled me through the dark heart of fever and nursed me back to health; and to her brother, Johnny Storm, who fought alongside my cousin, the Lady Tethys, in the name of Atlantis. While it is true that I have occasionally sparred with these four in the past, they have proven themselves noble comrades-in-arms, dedicated to upholding justice, no matter the circumstances!

"If you cheer for my return, then you must cheer for these courageous heroes, who have risked much to come to the aid of your prince!"

There was a pause as the assembled merhumans stared at the four helmeted surfacedwellers. Many had never laid eyes on a human before, much less such a strange creature as the

Thing. Then the crowd's voices joined as one, cheering and applauding.

Reed stretched his right arm ten feet high and waved it about in acknowledgment, while Ben took a deep, formal bow.

"All hail the Fantastic Four!"

A pretty little mermaiden darted forward and draped a lei made from plaited seaweed and sea-shells around Johnny's neck, batting her eyes coyly and giggling as she rejoined her school-mates. Johnny grinned from ear to ear.

"In addition to the Fantastic Four, I also wish to recognize the service of my cousin, the Lady Tethys. Although sorely used by her nefarious kinsman, the late and unlamented Lord Tydeus, Viscount of Charybdis, she proved her true loyalty to the crown. Unlike Baron Hiordis and Lord Seth, who were officers of the Atlantean Army and the Royal Guard, Tethys was but a young girl with no formal military training— yet this did not prevent her from organizing the guerilla resistance to Kreeg's reign of terror! By royal decree, I hereby order that the estate of Tydeus be bequeathed to her. As of this day, she is to be known as Lady Tethys, Viscountess Charybdis. And I hope that I will soon be given the honor and pleasure of announcing her betrothal to Baron Hiordis.''

The crowd began cheering again and Hiordis boosted Tethys onto his shoulders so that she could wave at her fellow Atlanteans. Sue smiled as she watched the young lovers parade about the Grand Plaza. ''She's quite beautiful. Don't you think, Reed?'' she asked.

''She's attractive enough, I suppose. But nowhere as beautiful as you,'' Reed said, taking his wife's hand in his.

''You silver-tongued devil! You always know what to say,'' Sue smiled. She leaned forward to kiss him, but was kept from doing so by their helmets. ''I can't wait until we're out of these suits!''

''You and me both,'' Reed chuckled, winking.

The official portion of the ceremony now over, Namor descended from the dais and moved to where the Fantastic Four stood.

''That was some speech, Subby,'' Ben said. ''You'd almost think you liked us.''

''I meant every word, Ben Grimm. You have done me a great service. I do not take such things lightly. The Fantastic Four may always count on the Sub-Mariner in times of trouble,''

Namor said, offering his hand. Reed took it without hesitation.

"We thank you, Namor. I'll have the serum synthesized within a few hours—there should be enough for your physicians to inoculate the entire citizenry of Atlantis."

"Good. I plan to make the serum available to Lemuria as well. Our kingdoms have warred against each other for centuries, but I have no desire to see their race wiped out so cruelly."

"Namor, what will become of Byrrah?" Sue asked.

Namor sighed and shook his head, smiling wryly. "I have the right to both condemn and pardon criminals—even those who would see me dead. In Byrrah's case, I have chosen to spare his life."

"I know he's yer blood relative an' all, Subby," Ben said. "But, aren't you bein' a little light on the guy? After all, he *did* try and have you rubbed out!"

"Prince Byrrah is not the villain Doom is. My cousin is not evil—merely weak. But even in his weakness he showed both strength and mercy. I have ordered him placed under house arrest for the rest of his natural life, which is punishment enough for one such as Byrrah. I

have forgiven my cousin much over the years—
and perhaps, in time, I will forgive him this.''

Sue smiled and touched Namor's hand.
''You're a good and kind ruler, Namor. And a
better cousin than Byrrah deserves.''

''What about that damn big lizard?'' Ben
asked. ''Are you sure you're not gonna need
some more help? I mean, are those boulders you
and I tossed on top of Cecil the Seasick Sea
Serpent gonna be enough to keep him down?''

''You needn't concern yourself with the Leviathan, Ben Grimm. Even as we speak, the
royal engineers are making their way to the
Valley of the Drowned Gods to erect a proper
capstone over the beast's resting place. The
power that binds the great serpent is god-born,
and as long as the Trident of Poseidon is in
place, the Leviathan will remain safely asleep.
Until the time he is needed.''

''Needed? What would you need that big
bruiser for?''

''The end of the world.''

''Huh?''

''The Leviathan is both the destroyer of Atlantis—and its vengeance. The great serpent
slumbers, awaiting the day when Atlantis can no
longer stand against the surface world. On that

dread day, the Trident is to be removed and the Horn of Triton smashed to pieces, and the Leviathan allowed to visit its wrath on the world. Seaquakes of cataclysmic proportions will rock the ocean floor, creating tsunamis large enough to drown Britain, Japan, even Australia, as Atlantis itself was overwhelmed, centuries before! Atlantis will be utterly destroyed as well, but we would die knowing our enemies had suffered losses as great as our own—perhaps greater. But I assure you, Ben Grimm, no Atlantean longs for that day. I respect you four immensely, but I know all too well that you are not representative of the surface world. Should I decide I have no choice, I will have no qualms about freeing the Leviathan. Tell that to your precious United Nations, Reed Richards.''

* * *

They were once more inside the F-4, headed toward home. Reed, already back in uniform, sat at the controls while the rest of the team unsuited.

''Man, am I glad t'get that fish bowl offa my everlovin' noggin!'' Ben rumbled as he removed his helmet. He glanced out the aft window, watching the spires and minarets of the sunken city gradually disappear. When he could no longer see Atlantis, he turned to face Reed.

"Hey, High Pockets—are you gonna tell those U.N. bozos what Subby told ya—about that Leviathan thingie bein' their doomsday weapon?"

"No, Ben, I'm not."

"Howcum? I mean—mebbe if those jerkolas knew that Namor had that kinda muscle in his favor, mebbe they'd be more willin' t'lissen to what he's got to say."

"Perhaps. And perhaps they'd feel so threatened, they'd move against Atlantis before Namor could use the Leviathan against them—thereby precipitating the very disaster they were so fearful of in the first place."

"I see yer point. I don't like it, but I see it. But what about the Sub-Mariner? You and I both know what a temper he's got. What if he decides to yank that oversized cocktail fork out—then what?"

"When and if that time comes, I seriously doubt the threat will start with Namor. Bear in mind—the Atlanteans have had the ultimate doomsday weapon for thousands of years—and they have yet to use it! We can only hope that the human race can also control itself that long."

"Amen t'that, Stretch," whispered the Thing as he looked out the observation window at the shimmering patterns made by the light filtering through the water. "Amen t'that."

NANCY A. COLLINS's first novel, *Sunglasses After Dark*, the first book in the Sonja Blue cycle, won the Horror Writers of America's Bram Stoker Award. From 1991–1993 she was the writer for DC Comics's *Swamp Thing* comic book, and now is responsible for the DC Vertigo series *Wick*. In 1989 and 1990, she was nominated for the Campbell Award, and in 1992 she was a nominee for the comic industry's Eisner Award. She is currently working on the next Sonja Blue book, as well as another novel and a collection of short stories.

PAUL RYAN is a New England–based cartoonist and a graduate of the Massachusetts College of Art. He worked as a graphic designer for eleven years, then as an assistant to then Marvel artist Bob Layton. In 1985 he struck out on his own, and his artwork has graced the pages of *Squadron Supreme*, *DP7* (which he cocreated with Mark Gruenwald), *Quasar*, *The Avengers*, *Avengers West Coast*, *Iron Man*, and *Ravage 2099* (which he cocreated with Stan Lee). He currently pencils and coplots (with Tom De-Falco) the monthly *Fantastic Four* comic, and also pencils the Sunday *Spider-Man* comic strip.

SPIDER-MAN®

__SPIDER-MAN: CARNAGE IN NEW YORK by David
Michelinie & Dean Wesley Smith   1-57297-019-7/$5.99
Spider-Man must go head-to-head with his most dangerous enemy,
Carnage, a homicidal lunatic who revels in chaos. Carnage has been
returned to New York in chains. But a bizarre accident sets Carnage
loose upon the city once again! Now it's up to Spider-Man to stop
his deadliest foe. *A collector's first edition*

__THE ULTIMATE SPIDER-MAN   0-425-14610-3/$12.00
Beginning with a novella by Spider-Man cocreator Stan Lee and Peter
David, this anthology includes all-new tales from established comics
writers and popular authors of the fantastic, such as: Lawrence Watt-
Evans, David Michelinie, Tom DeHaven, and Craig Shaw Gardner.
An illustration by a well-known Marvel artist accompanies each story.
Trade

__SPIDER-MAN: THE VENOM FACTOR by Diane Duane
1-57297-038-3/$5.99
In a Manhattan warehouse, the death of an innocent man points to
the involvement of Venom—the alien symbiote who is obsessed with
Spider-Man's destruction. Yet Venom has always safeguarded
innocent lives. Either Venom has gone completely around the bend,
or there is another, even more sinister suspect.

®TM and ©1995 Marvel Entertainment Group, Inc. All rights reserved.